Benjy's Ghost

Jacqueline Roy was born in London of Caribbean and English parentage. Her mother, Yvonne, was an actor, and her father, Namba, was a novelist, sculptor and painter. He was also a Maroon – a descendant of escaped slaves. The Maroons of Jamaica have always tried to keep up African traditions of living and working, and before he left Jamaica Jacqueline's father was the official storyteller and carver. Traditionally this role was passed from father to son, but Jacqueline wasn't going to let the fact that she was a girl prevent her from following in his footsteps. She says, "I wanted to tell stories ever since my father's death when I was seven years old. When I was growing up, there were very few books with black characters in them. I enjoyed reading more than anything else; I went to the library most days. But it was impossible back then to find any books about someone like me, a black girl who'd been born in Britain. I knew that if I wanted to read something like that, I'd have to write it myself."

Now a full-time lecturer in Post-colonial Literatures and Creative Writing at Manchester Metropolitan University, Jacqueline has written novels and short stories for both children and adults. Her books for younger readers include *Soul Daddy*, *Fat Chance*, *A Daughter Like Me* and *Playing It Cool*, as well as "Sunday Father", a short story in the Walker collection *Paying For It*.

Jacqueline loves eating ice cre̶͟͞ preferably at the same tim̶ her dog, on whom the cha̶

Benjy's Ghost

Jacqueline Roy

WALKER BOOKS
AND SUBSIDIARIES

LONDON • BOSTON • SYDNEY • AUCKLAND

First published 2004 by Walker Books Ltd
87 Vauxhall Walk, London SE11 5HJ

2 4 6 8 10 9 7 5 3 1

Text © 2004 Jacqueline Roy
Cover photographs: Jack Russell terrier: Jeffrey Braverman / Getty Images
Boy reading comic: Getty Images

This book has been typeset in Horley OS MT and Countryhouse

Printed in Great Britain by J.H. Haynes & Co. Ltd

British Library Cataloguing in Publication Data:
a catalogue record for this book is available from the British Library

ISBN 0-7445-9078-7

www.walkerbooks.co.uk

For Ann Germanacos, with grateful thanks for your friendship and support

one

At breakfast that morning, Benjy's father Andy said, "We'll be having a special tea tonight. I've got something to tell you. It's big, exciting news."

"Tell me now," Benjy pleaded, but his dad wouldn't budge. "Not until tonight," he insisted. "It's celebration time. I'll get in some Cokes and we'll order a pizza."

"Ice cream?" suggested Benjy hopefully. "My best flavour?"

"Sure thing," replied Andy. "Toffee Crunch it is."

Benjy smiled. It was good to have something nice to think about on a Monday morning. He was in Mrs Harris's class and he needed to forget how fed up that made him feel.

"Go next door and ask Steven if he wants a lift to school with us," said Andy.

Steven Jenkins was in Benjy's class and they were meant to be friends, but Benjy wasn't all that fond of him. Steven was too much of a scaredy cat for Benjy's liking. Even as he knocked on Steven's door, he knew he'd have left for school already. Benjy's dad was running late as usual and Steven hated being late. He wouldn't risk it for anything.

Sure enough, Mrs Jenkins opened the door and said, "Steven's gone, love. You're a bit late this morning. Tell your dad he won't need a lift this afternoon either because he's going to the dentist."

Benjy nodded and ran back indoors. "We're late, Dad, Steven's gone."

"I can't help that, Benjy. Where did I put my briefcase?"

"Come on, Dad. I'll get told off again. It isn't fair."

"Stop going on, Benjy, you're not helping. Just find my briefcase for me and then we can be off."

* * *

Mrs Harris did tell Benjy off, but she didn't seem quite as fierce as usual. Her eyes didn't go dark the way they usually did when she was cross, and she didn't tap her big feet at all.

"Just don't be late again this week, OK?" she said, and then told him to sit down, almost kindly. "Steven will fill you in on what we've been doing," she added. Was it Benjy's imagination, or did she actually smile as she said it?

Benjy hardly listened to Mrs Harris droning on that morning. His mind steamed through all kinds of exciting ideas. Maybe Dad had finally saved enough money for that trip to Disney World in Florida. It was Benjy's dream to go there. Or perhaps Mum was getting a divorce from her new husband and was coming back home from America to live in England.

"Benjy Dobson, pay attention please," Mrs Harris said.

Benjy looked up, expecting a long telling-off for not listening but it didn't come. Instead, Mrs Harris was looking at him in a rather strange way, as if she was actually worried about him or something. Benjy gave himself a mental shake. He and Mrs Harris were sworn enemies. Everything about him seemed to annoy her, from his untidy writing to his habit of being late for school. That wasn't his fault though. It was because his dad overslept. Dad could sleep through all four of the alarm clocks he set each night. "I work too hard, Benjy, that's the trouble," he'd say, and it was probably true. He always seemed to be working. He worked for social services and he even brought his files home with him and wrote things at the kitchen table while Benjy sat in the living-room watching TV. Benjy remembered the special meal they would be having that night and it made him smile. They hardly ever ate together. Dad was just too busy.

"How do you spell 'collection', Benjy?" Mrs Harris asked. "Come and write it on the board."

"C-o-r-r-e-c-k-s-h-u-n" wrote Benjy slowly.

Everybody laughed.

"I said 'collection'," said Mrs Harris, rolling her eyes. "And you haven't spelt 'correction' right either. You have to learn to pay attention, Benjy."

She went on and on about the same thing all the

time. Pay attention, Benjy. Pay attention. Benjy, you're not paying attention. He felt like saying he would pay attention if she wasn't so boring. She was the most boring teacher in the whole world. Yet, at the same time, there was something fascinating about her. She was weird, even for a teacher. Her clothes were usually bright yellow or purple. Her Afro hair was short, like Benjy's, but it had bits of red in it because she dyed it red on purpose. But the strangest thing about her, in Benjy's opinion, was her feet. They were enormous and she always wore huge white trainers, but not with trousers, with a skirt, so that they looked even bigger. Benjy secretly called her Big Foot.

She was scary. She could frown more fiercely than anyone he'd ever met. And when she told you off, it could be heard in the Infants on the other side of the road.

"Pay attention, Benjy," Mrs Harris boomed, making him jump. "What page are we on?"

Benjy took a guess. "Page seven?" he said.

"Page twenty-three. I do wish you would learn to pay attention."

Yet, even though Mrs Harris was shouting, she wasn't putting the usual effort into it. She was only operating at half the normal level of sound. Benjy looked at her and, for the second time that day, it seemed like she was smiling.

Benjy didn't understand it at all and he felt rather worried. He liked things to be the way they usually were. You knew where you were at school, mostly. Dinner was at quarter past twelve, and there were always chips on Fridays. Mrs Harris made you do arithmetic in the morning and you had to read a storybook every afternoon. You always went home at half past three, unless you had After School Club. Teachers were horrible. Other children were also pretty horrible, like Paul Fish, although there were some nice ones too – Steven Jenkins would be OK if he wasn't such a wuss. Altogether, it was ordinary – the same things every day. Benjy liked ordinary. He didn't like it when people started to behave in different ways. It almost made him feel ill, like he was being held by his heels and shaken hard in a topsy-turvy kind of way.

Benjy shook himself and decided he had to

stop worrying. He was going to turn into Steven Jenkins (who worried all the time) if he didn't watch out. Besides, he really didn't have time to worry about Mrs Harris almost being nice to him. He had more important things to think about. He was getting another wonderful idea about Dad's surprise. Two season tickets for City matches and a promise from Dad that they'd go every single time City were playing at home, however busy he was. And they'd be invited to visit the dressing-room afterwards and meet all the players. And they would be so impressed with Benjy – his dedication, his devotion to the team – that they'd give him a free leather football, signed with the names of every single player. And then they'd adopt him as their lucky mascot and he'd get to go to away matches on the coach with the team, and he'd have the best seat at every ground, right near the pitch, beside the reserves. And he'd bring them such luck. *And it's a wonderful goal for City! What a moment for the fans! It has to be the goal of the season! Their new mascot's certainly bringing a change of fortune for the team. It was a very lucky day indeed for City when they met young Benjy Dobson!*

"I'm not telling you again, Benjy, sit up straight and pay attention."

If only he could believe that Mrs Harris *wouldn't* be telling him again, but he knew she would, over and over again until the day ended. He couldn't wait to get away from her. "Half past three, half past three," he chanted to himself, as if saying it would bring it nearer.

He looked up. Mrs Harris was standing beside him now, but she was talking quietly and she was still looking almost kind. It was so confusing that Benjy decided he'd better pay attention for the rest of the morning.

At dinner time, Benjy sat by himself on the old broken bench. He wanted to play football with the others but Paul Fish, one of the big boys from Mr Jackson's class, was bossing everyone about as usual. He'd had it in for Benjy ever since he'd called him Fish Face. Well, what did he expect? If you had a name like Fish you were bound to get called things – people just couldn't help themselves.

Benjy decided to risk it and walked over to the group of boys, trying to look as if he didn't care whether they let him play or not. "Can I have a kick?" he said.

"No," said Paul, without even looking at him.

"Go on. You're a player short."

"No," said Paul again.

Benjy looked at Steven, but Steven just looked at the ground and said nothing. It wasn't fair. He hardly ever got to play and he was good at football. He really enjoyed playing too. One day, he'd be talent-spotted for City, or maybe even United. Benjy instantly felt ashamed of himself. It was an act of extreme betrayal even to think of Manchester's other team, let alone consider playing for them. The thought was such a bad one to have had that something terrible would probably happen now. Maybe Dad would have to work late and they wouldn't have the pizza. Maybe he'd even have to cancel the surprise. Benjy could have kicked himself. How stupid of him to have thought of United, just when he needed everything to go well.

"I don't want to play your stupid old game

anyway," Benjy told Paul. He snatched up the ball and kicked it as hard and as high as he could. Then he glared at Steven and walked back alone to the old broken bench.

"Benjy Dobson, you'll pay for that," shouted Paul, but Benjy wasn't all that scared. Paul was all mouth most of the time.

Mrs Harris came over. "Is everything all right, Benjy?" she said.

"Yes," he answered and, before she could sit down beside him, he got up and walked away. The last thing he needed was a teacher on his case, especially one like Mrs Harris. Benjy stood by the gate and leaned against the wall. Two hours and twenty minutes till home time, he thought. Not that he was counting or anything like that. And then, unless he'd jinxed it by thinking of United, he'd hear about his father's surprise.

two

When school finished, Benjy was amazed to see his dad waiting for him in the car. He'd imagined that thinking of United would have brought enough bad luck to make his father forget to do everything he promised for the next ten years. "Dad! You're here," he said.

Andy looked puzzled. "Of course I'm here."

"And the surprise – are we still having it?"

"Of course we are. Why wouldn't we be having it? Did you think I'd forget or something?"

Benjy didn't answer. He'd learned not to expect too much from his dad. He was a great dad in tons of ways, it was just that he had a terrible memory. He forgot loads of things all the time. He'd forgotten to collect Benjy from school once and it had been almost dark before he'd remembered. Benjy had been forced to stay in the head's office, making polite conversation and trying to pretend that he wasn't worried silly. He'd been afraid that his dad had left him forever, the way his mum had done. And when Andy had finally arrived, he hadn't even noticed how upset Benjy was and behaved as if everything was just the same as usual.

Benjy had forgiven him for it now, but it had taken a long time. Still, at least he had turned up today. "Can we have a Hawaiian pizza?" Benjy asked. They hardly ever had Hawaiian because his dad didn't like pineapple or ham, but some-times, on special occasions, he was willing to eat it anyway.

"Oh, go on then. Hawaiian it is."

Benjy ordered the pizza from the car, using his father's mobile, to cut down the waiting time. He was starving. "Did you get the Coke?" he asked as the car pulled up outside the house.

Andy nodded.

"And the ice cream?"

"Best quality Toffee Crunch. And I've got

The Last Action Hero out on DVD – your favourite film."

It had been Benjy's favourite once, when he was about seven. He'd grown out of it now, and besides, he knew it off by heart. But his dad had given in about the pizza and Benjy didn't want to spoil the evening by showing he was disappointed.

"Lay the table, Benjy, there's a good boy," said Andy as they went inside the house.

"Dad!"

"Listen, I've had a long, hard day. It's not much to ask."

"Can't we have it on our lap in front of the telly?"

"No. I want to tell you the news. I can't do that with the television on."

"You can. I will listen, I promise."

"Let's have some quiet in the house, just for once."

Benjy laid the table silently. Dad was talking about surprises, yet he was sounding serious, as if it was bad news, not good. Benjy had that familiar topsy-turvy feeling again, the one he'd had that morning when Mrs Harris had almost been nice to him.

The pizza arrived piping hot; they didn't even need to warm it in the oven. Benjy gulped down some Coke and felt happy again.

"Ben, something pretty amazing's happened," said his dad suddenly. "I've found someone."

What did he mean, *found* someone? "I didn't know anyone was lost," said Benjy.

"No, listen, Benjy. You know how unhappy I was when your mother married Rob and went to live in America?"

Benjy nodded. They'd both been pretty unhappy since then.

"Well, I've always thought that if I could find somebody else too, it would make a big difference, get me on track again. And I have found someone and I've asked her to marry me."

Benjy felt as if he was dreaming. It couldn't be happening. All the predictable, ordinary things were suddenly topsy-turvy again. It was as if snow was falling in summer.

"You can't marry anybody else. You're married to Mum."

"We're divorced now, Ben. We've been divorced for three years, you know that."

"You're still married."

"Not any more. Look, it won't change anything, not really. We're staying in this house. Carol will be moving in here, with her daughter—"

"Her daughter?"

"I know I should have done this differently. I should have told you about Carol and Kayla sooner. Well, you know Carol, of course, but you haven't met Kayla yet—"

"I don't want to meet her, not ever!"

"This has been a shock. I knew it would be. I just didn't know how to tell you about it. I don't want a lot of trouble from you, Benjy. Work's hard at the moment and I've got a lot of stress to deal with. I just want you to be happy and good. I don't want tantrums or temper. I can't deal with that right now."

Benjy felt like chucking the pizza all over his dad's head, and following that with a shower of Coke, but he didn't because he was too stunned. He couldn't take it in. He was getting a stepmother, like in *Snow White*. She was bound to be a poisoner of some description. He'd have to lay off apples, for a while at least. And then there was the daughter. A girl in the house. It was too horrible to imagine.

"Benjy, are you listening?" said Dad.

"I'm never going to listen to you again. I hate you! Two people coming to live here that I don't even know."

"Benjy, I've told you, Carol *is* someone you know. In fact, you see her every day."

Benjy wondered who Dad meant. Who did he see every day? There was the woman in the sweet shop, of course. Things began to look up. She'd bring a lifetime's supply of chocolate. And then there was the woman Dad worked with – the one whose husband had died. She always let Benjy have her son's computer games once he'd got bored with them, and some of them were really, really good… Only she wasn't called Carol, and she had a son, and Carol had a daughter… "How old is Kayla?"

"A year younger than you. Benjy, listen to me. It's Carol Harris. I've asked Mrs Harris to marry me, and she's said yes. Benjy, sit down, eat the rest of your pizza. *Benjy!*"

A fizz of Coke exploded across the table and was followed by the pizza and its box. Benjy knew that he would be without TV for at least a fortnight for making such a mess and that there would be no sweets or comics for even longer, but he didn't care. His dad deserved more than a helping of pizza on his head. Mrs Harris of all people! She was a monster and a witch and Benjy couldn't believe that she was actually moving in with them. It was bad enough to see her all the time at school, but now she'd be in Benjy's house as well, bossing him about, making him behave himself every hour of the day.

three

Benjy had known that something had been going on for weeks. His dad had skulked around as if he'd had a big secret. He had been out every other night, leaving Benjy with Mrs Jenkins and Steven. Benjy hadn't enjoyed it very much. Steven liked reading by himself and he didn't talk that much. Benjy preferred watching TV or playing outside. When he'd seen his dad the following day, he'd always been given a present – a toy car or his favourite bubble gum (the one with the cards to collect) to make up for Andy being away. It never made up for it though.

Benjy was used to grown-ups behaving secretively. It had happened all the time just before his mother had left. Night after night over the past few weeks, Benjy had lain in his bed, worrying about what was happening. He'd been too scared of the answer to try to discover what was going on. And now the secret was out. His dad was getting married, and to Mrs Harris of all people! It was worse than he could ever have imagined.

Benjy curled up into a little ball and squeezed himself into the tiny space between the cupboard and the wall. He felt safe there. He stretched out his arm and pulled Edgar, his teddy bear, from the bed. He held him tight, even though he knew that he wasn't a baby any more. The bear was warm and furry and comforting.

I should have seen the signs, thought Benjy. He remembered all the times that Dad had stood up for Mrs Harris when Benjy had criticized her. "She's a very good teacher," he had said, or "I'm sure she likes you a lot really, Benjy."

Dad probably liked Mrs Harris more than anyone else in the whole world. That's what it was like when you married someone. You had to love them best. It was in the rules. Mrs Harris would be number one for Dad now. And Benjy would be number two. Or maybe even number three if that daughter Kayla muscled in ahead of him. It was really, really depressing.

"Are you coming downstairs, Benjy?" called his father.

"No," Benjy answered crossly.

"Suit yourself," came the reply.

Benjy remained hidden for what seemed like hours. Eventually his father came knocking at the door. "Can I come in?" he asked.

"No," said Benjy, but Andy came in anyway.

"Come out of the corner, Benjy," he said, holding out his hand.

"No."

"It's a bit of a tight squeeze in there, especially when Edgar's in there too."

Benjy was embarrassed. His dad would think he was being a baby. "Edgar forced his way in here with me. I didn't want him to come."

"No, of course you didn't," his dad replied, as if he believed it. "I'm sorry I didn't prepare you better for the news about me and Carol. I just didn't want you to be upset."

"It's worse because you didn't tell me."

"I know, I can see that now. Come downstairs, please, Benjy. We could watch that serial you like, the one about the school."

Benjy crawled out of the corner and followed his dad downstairs. At least he wasn't going to be punished for throwing the pizza last night. But as he watched TV, he kept remembering that Mrs Harris was moving into his house and he nearly cried with the tragedy of it.

For the next few days, Benjy and his father behaved as if the wedding wasn't happening. It wasn't even mentioned between them. For a while, Benjy hoped that his dad had realized how upset he was at the very thought of it and had called it off, but then on the way to school he said, "I've invited Carol and Kayla round this evening."

Steven was in the car too and Benjy could see his ears pricking up. The last thing he wanted was for everyone to know that his Dad was marrying a teacher. He imagined Paul Fish going on and on about it, calling him Teacher's Pet and goodness knows what else. He glared at his father, willing him to stop, but he didn't get the hint. "It will be a chance for you to see Carol out of school," he added. "She won't be the same with you, Benjy. She'll be more like a friend once you're both out of the classroom."

Benjy found it hard to think of Mrs Harris having any friends at all, let alone count himself as one of them. He almost laughed out loud, it seemed so ridiculous.

"Did I tell you that Carol's got a dog? His name's Jonah and he'll be coming to live with us too."

"I don't like dogs," said Benjy.

"Yes you do, you know you do. You've always said we ought to get one."

"Well, I won't like their dog. Just be quiet, Dad. I can't hear myself think."

"Cheeky monkey," replied his dad, but he didn't say anything more.

"What was your dad talking about just then?" asked Steven as Andy dropped them at the school gate. "Who's Carol? Why's she moving in with you?"

"Mind your own business," said Benjy.

Steven looked sad and disappointed, so Benjy tried to be nice. "It's something private. I might tell you sometime but not yet, OK?"

Steven nodded. At least Benjy hadn't got angry or thrown anything, which made a change. Steven often thought that they might be best friends if Benjy didn't have such a temper. You never knew where you were with him. He could bite your head off for no reason. Steven was a bit scared of him and it was hard to like someone you were scared of.

In class, Benjy was even crosser and more difficult than usual. He kept dropping his pencils and books on purpose. And he slammed the door as he went out at play time. Mrs Harris didn't say a word. Benjy could tell that she was holding herself in. It was a wonder she didn't explode with the effort. Her mouth was tight and her eyes were bright with anger.

She would probably tell his father when she came round that evening. Teachers were such sneaks. You had to play them up, you didn't have a choice, and he had even more reason to play Mrs Harris up now that she was going to take his dad away from him. She was a big fat pig, thought Benjy.

He stood on his own in the playground, as he so often did, and watched the others playing. Steven was bouncing his ball so Benjy went up to him and snatched it away.

"Benjy!"

"I'm just playing," Benjy said. "Here, catch!"

Steven caught the ball and sent it back to Benjy. He wasn't very good at throwing and catching; he tended to drop the ball a lot. They began to play a catching game, bouncing the ball against the wall. "Concentrate, then!" said Benjy as Steven fumbled yet another catch.

"I *am* concentrating," Steven said. Anyone would think that Benjy was a teacher or something, the way he carried on. Steven wanted to say that he'd had enough now and didn't want to play any more, but he knew that Benjy wouldn't stand for that so he carried on running and throwing, even though he was red in the face and out of breath with the effort.

Benjy felt better after chucking a ball about with Steven, but once break was over and they went back into class he felt gloomy again. Mrs Harris put a load of sums on the board and then told Benjy off when he got some of them wrong. "You need to pay more attention," she said. "You're a clever boy but you don't bother to use that brain of yours."

Once again, Benjy tried to imagine what it would be like to live in the same house as Mrs Harris, but his imagination wouldn't stretch that far.

The day dragged but Benjy escaped from school at last. He hardly spoke to his dad or Steven on the drive home. As soon as he got in, he ran upstairs to his room. He lined his toy cars across the floor according to size, then kicked them into the wall. The crashing noise made him feel better. He picked them up and lined them up again, noticing the newly made dents and scratches. Well, he didn't care, they were old cars anyway.

"What are you doing, Benjy?" his dad called from downstairs. "Are you in your room?"

Benjy didn't answer. Where else would he be? He heard his father's footsteps on the stairs. "Go away, Dad," said Benjy, as Andy came into his bedroom.

His dad ignored this and sat beside him. "Listen, I know you're unhappy about Carol and Kayla coming this evening but you have to make the best of it. I'm not changing my mind about the wedding so you need to get to know them properly."

Benjy could hardly believe it. Didn't his feelings even count? "You can't get married, Dad. It isn't fair. I don't want you to."

"I know you don't. I wish you didn't have such a thing about teachers. Can't you try not to make a fuss about this, just for me? You know how stressed I am at work. I can't take it from you, Benjy. I get enough ructions from the clients."

"Grown-ups are supposed to deal with ructions," said Benjy. "It's what you're for."

Andy rubbed Benjy's hair and laughed. "Well, funnily enough, mate, I see grown-ups rather differently. For a start, not always as the enemy. We can help from time to time."

"That's what I mean. You're supposed to help. Deal with ructions, deal with fuss."

"I don't have the patience of a saint. I wish I did, because then it would be so much easier for us to get on."

"Benjy leaned against his father. "We do get on, Dad. That's just it. We get on great, and we won't get on any more, not now they're coming to live with us."

"We'll get on, same as we always have. You're my son. You come first."

"No I don't, or you wouldn't be marrying Big Foot."

"Benjy."

"Well, I don't. I don't come first with you or Mum. Look what happened when she met that Robert. She hardly even phones me any more."

"It's expensive, phoning from America."

"I don't care. I should be worth the money."

"You are, Ben."

"Seems like it."

"I wouldn't be doing any of this if I really thought you'd be unhappy."

"What do I have to do to convince you?"

His dad laughed again.

"Don't laugh at me!" said Benjy.

"I'm not really laughing at you, Benjy. I'm just remembering something Mrs Harris – Carol – said. She really likes you. She says you have a lot of spirit."

"She might say that to you. All she says to me is 'Pay attention, Benjy,' or 'Stop being such a silly boy.'"

"Carol doesn't do favourites, you know that. If you're naughty, you have to take the consequences, same as every other boy or girl in the class."

Benjy laughed sarcastically. "Favourites? As if! I'm the person she hates most in the entire universe."

"Don't exaggerate."

"OK, the entire planet then."

"Anyway, I'm sure you'll like Kayla, even if it's hard for you to get on with Carol."

"I don't want to meet her."

"She's a nice little girl. You'll get on great with her."

"She's only seven."

"You're only eight."

Benjy rolled his eyes. Seven-year-olds were like infants compared to grown-up people of eight – it was obvious. "Anyway, she's a girl."

"She plays football. She loves it. And there's lots more you have in common, I promise you."

"I don't want to meet her, OK?"

But it seemed that Benjy didn't have a choice. Kayla arrived just before six. Mrs Harris was with her.

"Hello, Benjy," Mrs Harris said.

Benjy looked down. He wasn't even going to speak to her. She didn't deserve it. It wasn't like she could punish him for it. They weren't at school now.

"Benjy," said his dad, in his best warning voice.

"Hello," said Kayla, all smiles and politeness.

Benjy looked at her. She was pretty and neat and girly. She was wearing a pale yellow pina-fore dress and matching socks, with a pink and brown T-shirt underneath. She looked like an ice-cream sundae.

"Why don't you take Kayla upstairs?" said Andy.

"I don't want to," said Benjy.

"Upstairs," said his father, using the warning voice again.

Benjy went up, dragging his feet. Kayla trailed behind. Benjy dashed into his bedroom and shut the door before she could reach it. He leaned against it. "You're not coming in my room," he said.

"I don't even want to," said Kayla from the other side of the closed door. "It probably stinks, just like you."

"I don't want you living in this house. It's my house, not yours."

"You think I want to come? Think again, you stupid boy. But we don't have any choice."

Benjy grunted. There would be a choice if he had anything to do with it. This was war and he was determined to fight to the finish.

four

Benjy's dad and Mrs Harris had a small wedding service at a registry office. They didn't have a honeymoon because Andy was too busy. Benjy was glad about that – if his dad had gone away on top of everything else, he wouldn't have been able to stand it.

Mrs Harris, Kayla and Jonah the dog moved in the day after the wedding. As soon as the three of them arrived, they seemed to fill the place. Benjy flattened himself against the wall by the living-room door and wondered how he was going to stand it. "Say hello to Carol," said Benjy's dad, in his "let's all be happy" voice.

"Hello, Mrs Harris."

"I'm not Mrs Harris any more, Benjy. Besides,

I've told you, call me Carol when we're at home."

Benjy tried to say the word but it wouldn't come out. She would always be Mrs Harris to him, and her place was at school, beside her desk, holding a box of rubbers and pencils. She wasn't meant to be here in Benjy's own house, looking as if she owned the place.

"Say hello to Kayla," Mrs Harris instructed.

Benjy muttered something and stared hard at Kayla, trying to make her blush, but she just stared back even harder. Benjy saw with horror that she supported United. She was wearing a brand-new United shirt. It was so new that it still had the tag on; it dangled down Kayla's back like a necklace that had been put on the wrong way round. Perhaps she was letting it hang there on purpose so everyone would know how new her shirt was and how much it had cost. Benjy always covered his ears whenever United was mentioned, but he still knew that the latest United strip had only been on sale for a couple of weeks. And Kayla had it already. Mrs Harris was always saying that children should never be spoiled. It was obvious that she spoiled her own child rotten. The tag said £34.99. Mrs Harris had paid that much for a stupid United shirt. Benjy scowled at his dad, remembering that he had refused to fork out for a City shirt for him. He said it was far too expensive, even though City kits were cheaper than United ones.

"Say hello to Jonah," said Kayla, picking up the dog and holding him under Benjy's nose. "Give him a kiss."

Benjy pulled a face and backed away.

"Why don't you show Kayla her room, Benjy?" said Andy.

Benjy opened his mouth to tell his dad that she could find her own room, but the warning look on his father's face caused him to change his mind. "OK," he said, grudgingly, "come on, Kayla."

The grown-ups exchanged relieved glances, as if to say they knew all the changes would work out all right. "That's what they think," said Benjy under his breath. He turned to Kayla and said, "Put the dog down. It isn't allowed upstairs."

"Who says it isn't?"

"My dad says, that's who."

Andy muttered something to Mrs Harris, who muttered something back. Then he said, "I want Kayla to feel at home. I'm sure it wouldn't hurt if the dog went upstairs now and then."

"But you said—" began Benjy.

"I know I said I didn't want him on the beds, but I'm sure he's a well-behaved dog, isn't he, Kayla?"

"He's very well behaved," Kayla answered, and she began to follow Benjy upstairs, the dog bounding after her.

As they reached the landing, Benjy turned to her and said, "Dad's painted your room yellow. I think yellow's a horrible colour. It's the colour of cat sick."

Kayla made being sick noises and giggled, which surprised Benjy. He'd expected her to be cross. "It looks really disgusting," he added, assuming that she hadn't got the point.

"I like disgusting things," said Kayla with pride in her voice.

"You must love yourself then," said Benjy, pleased with his own quick humour.

"No, I love you," said Kayla, planting a big kiss on Benjy's cheek. He squealed and rubbed it hard, almost taking the skin off. "That's disgusting," he said.

"What did I tell you?" Kayla replied. "Disgusting is what I do best."

"Could have told you that," said Benjy.

Kayla tried to kick him on the shin, but he moved aside so fast that she grazed the landing wall instead.

"Dad, Kayla's kicking the wall," shouted Benjy.

"I'm not!" shouted Kayla.

"Be quiet, Benjy," said Andy.

"Be quiet, Kayla," said Carol.

"Telltale," said Kayla to Benjy.

"Here's your room. It's next to Dad's big bedroom where your mum's going to be as well. Dad didn't want you to be lonely. 'Poor little Kayla,' he said. 'She won't want to feel as if she's all by herself in a strange new house.'"

"I can take care of myself," said Kayla, entering the room with a swagger that was meant to look grown up. Benjy thought it looked rather pathetic. He could swagger much better than that.

He could swagger like a pirate.

Kayla's things had already arrived. They had come in a van earlier that morning. The boxes were piled high in Kayla's new room. Jonah leaped over one and found himself a warm seat by the radiator. Kayla clambered after him and sat on the floor, stroking his coat. He was a dark-brown shaggy dog with a squashed nose and paws that were too big for his small body.

"What kind of dog is he?" asked Benjy.

"The best kind," said Kayla.

"No, I meant what make is he?"

"Dogs aren't makes, they're breeds. He's nothing in particular. Mum says he's a very fine mixture."

"Mixture of what?"

Kayla shrugged. "What does it matter? He's just a great dog. He loves to chase balls. He runs so fast, sometimes he can hardly stop. He's the fastest runner ever. If there was a dog Olympics he'd win for sure."

"He looks like a stupid ugly thing to me."

"Well you look like a stupid ugly thing to him."

Benjy stared at Kayla. She was pretty good at

the smart remarks. He'd thought he was the king of sarcasm but she was running him a close second. Benjy wasn't sure whether to be excited by the challenge or furious with her for being so lippy.

Kayla began to open the boxes that surrounded her. She brought out a collection of United magazines and posters.

"You're not putting those on the wall. They'll pollute the whole house."

"I am," said Kayla. "You can't stop me."

Benjy reached up to snatch one of the posters from Kayla's hand. Jonah growled menacingly.

"He doesn't like it when someone tries to hurt me or Mum," said Kayla.

"I wasn't trying to hurt you. I was only trying to stop you putting up the poster," said Benjy anxiously. Jonah had big teeth. "Oh, put it up if you want to. What do I care? United have had their day. It's City's turn now."

"In your dreams," said Kayla.

Benjy wondered how Kayla knew that he dreamed of City's future victories almost every night. "The tag's showing on your shirt," he said. "You look really stupid."

Kayla looked embarrassed but she just lifted the shirt over her head and removed the tag with her teeth.

"At least City doesn't rip off the fans, not like United who make you pay an arm and a leg for a stupid shirt," said Benjy.

"You really like the word stupid, don't you? You need to widen your vocabulary. That's what Mum says. You should write down a new word every day and learn it. I always do."

Benjy just stared. He couldn't think of an answer to that. Then he said, "She spoils you rotten, doesn't she? A new United shirt already."

"She didn't buy it for me," Kayla said. "It was a present from your dad."

"I don't believe you."

"Ask him then. He'll tell you. He bought it for me on the day the new strip came out."

"He wouldn't. He says they're too expensive."

"Ask him," said Kayla.

Benjy ran downstairs. "Dad!" he shouted.

"Yes, what is it?" answered Andy. He was in the kitchen with his arm round Mrs Harris.

Benjy could hardly get the words out. "Kayla says you bought her that United shirt she's wearing."

"I wanted her to feel better about coming to live here. It's a big change for her, you know."

"It's a big change for me too, but you didn't buy me a City shirt. You said you wouldn't."

"I'm not made of money, Benjy."

"No, but you can buy things for her. Why can't you buy them for me? It isn't fair. You're horrible. I really hate you!"

Mrs Harris came towards him. "Benjy, don't get upset, your dad didn't mean to leave you out, it was just a mistake. I'll get you a City shirt first thing tomorrow."

"I don't want you to buy me a shirt. I don't want anything from you. I hate all of you, you're nothing but big fat stupid ugly pigs!" shouted Benjy, running back upstairs to his room.

He sat on the floor with his dented cars and thought about the glory of owning a new City shirt. Perhaps he shouldn't have been so quick to turn down Mrs Harris's offer, but he hadn't been able to stop himself. You shouldn't accept presents from your enemies – it was obvious. Yet as soon as Benjy thought it, he realized that his argument didn't make much sense. It would be much better to get your enemies to pay for everything. You could make them spend so much that they became absolutely bankrupt and then you could laugh and laugh when they ran out of all their money.

Benjy opened his bedroom door again and ran downstairs. He sat beside Mrs Harris at the kitchen table. "You can get me the shirt, if you like," he said.

"It's a deal, Benjy," she replied.

Benjy smiled to himself. She was falling into his trap so easily. Sometimes people were really stupid. It was lucky he was so clever. This way he would get his new shirt and Mrs Harris would suffer because she had to pay for it. Things were definitely looking up.

five

Benjy had thought that Mrs Harris or even Kayla would be the biggest pests in his house but Jonah turned out to be an even larger problem. He was smelly, especially when he was wet, and everything about him irritated Benjy, from his madly wagging tail to the way his tongue hung out when he got too hot. He bounced everywhere and he trampled on all kinds of things with muddy paws; some of Benjy's best City magazines now had big paw prints right across the centre pages. To make matters worse, the others thought Jonah could do no wrong. Even his dad thought he was wonderful, and Kayla and Mrs Harris were completely besotted by him. Whenever Benjy tried to tell him off, everyone said in a loud chorus, "Leave that poor dog alone, Benjy. What's he ever done to you?"

When Benjy came home from school, he had to take the mutt out for a walk, even if it was pouring with rain. He missed most of his favourite TV programmes. Kayla never had to take him out because she always had piano lessons or dancing classes or acting club. The unfairness of life was really starting to get to Benjy.

Yet the funny thing was, Jonah seemed to like him. He started following Benjy around, which made him crosser than ever. "Go away, you stupid dog," Benjy would say whenever Jonah scratched at his bedroom door to be let in. He couldn't even go to the toilet without Jonah trying to follow him.

"That dog's got no brains," Benjy said to Kayla one evening. He was trying to avoid the word stupid.

"He's highly intelligent. Everybody says so. If he could talk he'd win 'Mastermind' or 'University Challenge'."

"He's stupid," said Benjy.

Kayla picked him up on it at once. "Widen your vocabulary, you foolish boy," she said.

"You're a big fat pig," answered Benjy, walking away from her.

Kayla just laughed, which made him even crosser.

In the evenings, after tea, Mrs Harris would sit with Jonah on her lap. She didn't look nearly so fierce then. She would talk to the dog in a soft, kind voice, and stroke him behind his ears. Jonah would lay back, waving his paws in the air in a state of pure happiness.

Even his dad would purposely leave bits of fish or meat on his plate so that Jonah would get an after-dinner treat. And he bought him a brand-new ball. "He loves chasing games, doesn't he? You'll be able to throw this for him now, Benjy."

"Gee thanks," Benjy said. "Just what I always wanted." How come everyone in the house, even the bloomin' dog, was getting presents from his father, while he got absolutely nothing? He had to be the unluckiest boy in the universe.

*　*　*

One morning, as Benjy was eating his breakfast, his father said, "There's a letter here for you. It's from your mother."

Benjy took it eagerly. As soon as he could leave the table, he ran upstairs and sat on his bed. He opened the letter very carefully. He didn't want to damage it – it was far too precious.

He read it slowly. Then he read it again, just in case there had been some mistake. But no, it was true. His mum was having another baby, someone who would take Benjy's place. He probably wouldn't even be her son any more. It wasn't as if he even got to see her now that she had moved to America. She'd forget him completely once the new baby was born.

Benjy thought he was going to cry but he held the tears back. He wasn't a baby, he was eight now and eight-year-olds didn't cry, no matter what. He jumped up and knocked all the books off the shelves and onto the floor. Then he stamped on them, crumpling the pages. "I hate you!" he shouted, to no one in particular.

His dad came running upstairs. "What now?" he said.

Benjy flung himself at his father, still deter-mined not to cry. "It's not fair, it's not fair," he kept repeating.

"What isn't fair, Benjy?" Andy said in a weary voice.

"She's going to have a baby."

"Your mother? Well, I wish she'd told me first. I could have prepared you for the news."

"That wouldn't have changed anything. She'd still be having it, wouldn't she?"

His dad took the letter and read it for himself.

"It's true, isn't it? I haven't got it wrong."

"No, you haven't got it wrong. Sandra is expecting a baby."

"This is so not fair!"

Andy put his arm around his son. "Ben, it doesn't have to be bad news. It could be some-thing really good. Do you remember when you were little? You always said how much you wanted a younger brother or sister. Now you're going to have one."

"I won't ever see her again. She'll be too busy with the new baby."

"I'm sure she'll make time for you. No matter

what happens, you're her oldest child and the first is always special, I promise."

"She doesn't even come to see me now so how is she going to come when the baby's here?"

"She'd really like to come, she just doesn't have the money. Robert lost his job two or three months ago and they're struggling to make ends meet—"

"It's just an excuse. She'd find a way to see me if she really wanted to."

"It's not as simple as that, Benjy."

"Why can't nice things ever happen any more? Why is it bad news all the time?"

"I know it seems like that at the moment, but nice things *are* happening, Benjy. In fact, I thought we'd go to the seaside at the weekend, as a treat. The weather forecast says it's going to be one of the hottest days of the year on Saturday."

"Just me and you?"

"No, everyone."

"Couldn't it be just us?"

"No, Benjy, me and you and Kayla and Carol are a family now. We need to do things together."

"But I want to spend some time with you."

"We will. We'll have a whole evening to ourselves very soon."

"When?"

"Maybe next week, or the week after, when I'm not so busy. But I'd like us to do the weekend trip as a family. We haven't done anything together yet and it might help to settle things down, get you and Kayla used to one another. We'll take swimming stuff and a picnic and we'll play games. Do you fancy cricket? And we'll do a cliff-top walk. It'll be great, I promise you."

Benjy didn't like walks, and he especially didn't like them when it was hot. And the countryside was boring, even when you were by the sea, unless there was a funfair or something. "Do we have to?" said Benjy.

"Come on, you know you'll really enjoy it once we get there. You can swim in the sea and everything. It will help to take your mind off things."

But Benjy didn't enjoy it, not in the least. It was boiling. The sun didn't let up for a minute and there was no breeze. And they were traipsing along this craggy bit of countryside through mud and cow pats as if it was supposed to be the best fun ever.

"When can we go back to the car?" Benjy kept asking.

"Be quiet, Ben, it's a lovely day. We're here to enjoy ourselves."

"But I'm not enjoying it," Benjy replied.

"I'm sure you are really, Benjy," said Mrs Harris. "Kayla loves it, don't you, Kayla?"

Kayla smiled happily and skipped along beside her mother. Benjy trailed behind with Jonah, who kept pausing to sniff out foxholes and badger droppings. He thought about his mother and the new baby, and the idea that he might never see her again.

"Why don't you throw Jonah's new ball for him?" said his dad.

"It's too hot."

"We'll go down to the beach soon," Mrs Harris said. "We'll all be able to cool off with a swim, even Jonah. He loves swimming."

"I hate swimming," said Benjy.

"You don't," Andy answered. "You're just

saying that because you're in a mood."

"He's been in a mood all his life," Kayla said. The grown-ups laughed cruelly.

"I am not in a mood!" shouted Benjy. He hated everyone, especially his mother. And most of all, he hated the new brother or sister he was about to have. He picked up the red ball and tossed it higher and further than he'd ever thrown anything before. It hit the ground and then bounced at an angle, seeming to gather speed all the while. Jonah gave an excited yelp and chased after it, his paws barely touching the grass. He was almost falling over himself in his rush to get to the ball. He ran faster and faster as the ball sped on, just in front of him.

Benjy held his breath. He could see what was going to happen next. Jonah wasn't thinking about anything except getting that ball. It was rolling towards the edge of the cliff. Jonah was still running after it. He was running too fast to stop.

"The cliff!" shouted Kayla.

Benjy stared at Jonah. The stupid dog was still running as fast as ever. He wasn't braking at all.

Benjy closed his eyes, hoping he was wrong. He opened them again. The ball was still speeding towards the cliff's edge and Jonah was still speeding after it.

"Stop!" Mrs Harris shouted in her loudest playground voice, but Jonah just kept on running. And then he was over the edge, soaring through the air like a bird in flight. If it hadn't been so awful it would have been a wonderful sight. Jonah was flying with the ball in his mouth, his ears flapping like wings, and then, with a single desperate yelp, he was gone.

There was a dreadful silence.

Everyone ran to the edge of the cliff. There was a small brown shape way down in the distance, lying perfectly still. "He's probably all right," said Benjy, full of false hope. "He's just playing dead."

"He isn't all right!" shouted Kayla. "How could he possibly still be alive after a fall like that? You've killed our dog, you rotten little brat, and no one will ever forgive you!"

SiX

There was no doubt that Jonah had gone forever. He had fallen at least seventy feet. There was no point in anyone going down to the bottom of the cliff. The sea was already starting to cover the beach below. Benjy could hardly believe it had happened. It was terrible.

They drove home in silence, except for Mrs Harris who sniffed every now and then and blew her nose into a large handkerchief. A tear rolled down her cheek. *Mrs Harris crying!* Benjy had that topsy-turvy feeling again.

"I suppose it was asking for trouble to call a dog Jonah," she said as they let themselves into the house.

"Why was it asking for trouble to call him

Jonah?" asked Kayla in a wobbly voice.

"I told you when we named him, Jonah was someone from the Bible who had a lot of bad luck."

Benjy thought about what had happened on the cliff. You're not wrong there, he decided. The stupid mutt shouldn't have followed the ball. Any other dog would have known to put the brakes on. Benjy had said this repeatedly since the accident, but everyone, even his own dad, said how cruel and unfeeling he was, so now he only thought it. Benjy sighed. He felt guilty and mean and miserable, though he was determined not to show it, unlike this lot, who were *all* crying now – even his dad. They didn't seem at all embarrassed. The sight of everybody bawling brought tears to Benjy's own eyes but he hastily brushed them away. He wasn't crying for Jonah, he told himself. He was tougher than that. He was crying because everybody hated him. Kayla called him Dog Killer under her breath. She'd probably paint the words on his bedroom door in red and no one would even tell her off for it.

It was tea time but Kayla, Andy and Mrs Harris all said they didn't feel like eating. Benjy couldn't understand it. He hadn't had a thing since the picnic and that was hours ago, so he was really hungry now. Everyone sat in the living-room but they didn't even turn on the television. OK, it was a shame about the dog but everyone being miserable and starving to death wasn't going to bring him back, was it?

Benjy put his hand in the biscuit tin. All he could find were a few boring pieces of short-cake. He'd hoped for chocolate biscuits. Hadn't Mrs Harris bought some on Thursday? Benjy was going to ask her where they were but he decided against it. He didn't want to remind her of his presence. She would only have a go at him again and tell him what a thoughtless boy he was.

Benjy filled his pockets with pieces of short-cake and went out into the garden. The sun was going in. He sat on the swing that his dad had put up when he was four. He swung as high as he could for a few minutes and then slowed down to a slight rock and ate some more biscuits. As he looked around him, he could almost see Jonah running through the grass. At that time of day he would have been hoping for an extra walk. He would have been sniffing round Benjy, trying to persuade him to take him out. For a moment, Benjy almost missed the stupid mutt.

And then it happened. Benjy caught a glimpse of Jonah sniffing round the cherry tree. He dug his heels into the ground and stopped the swing dead. He had to be imagining it. He rubbed his eyes. Then he looked again. There was Jonah, but he didn't look the same as he'd done before he'd gone over the cliff. No, this Jonah was shadowy and pale, like a bad photograph, but he was moving steadily round the tree and digging the earth with his paws.

"Jonah!" called Benjy, running towards him, but even as he caught up with the shadowy figure, Jonah disappeared again.

Benjy sat down on the grass where Jonah had just been. He must be going a bit crazy. Perhaps it was the guilt. He pushed another biscuit into his mouth to stop his stomach rumbling. A spot of rain fell on his hand and then another and another. It was no good. Benjy knew he couldn't stay outside any longer. He had to go indoors and get told off by everyone again.

The living-room was empty though, and the TV had been switched off. Benjy listened. He could hear Kayla playing music in her room and the low voice of his father talking to Mrs Harris in their bedroom. They were probably telling each other what a naughty boy he was.

Benjy decided he might as well make some toast. Food always made him feel better when things were going wrong. He got some bread out and put it into the toaster. Just as he was buttering the toast, he jumped in fright. There, in front of him, was Jonah again – shadowy, unreal Jonah, come back to haunt the living daylights out of him.

Benjy screamed and started to shake, dropping the toast butter-side down. Everyone came running downstairs.

"What is it?" asked Andy. "What's the matter?"

"It's Jonah, he's here. *Look!*"

Everyone looked towards the corner where Benjy was pointing.

"What are you talking about?" said Mrs Harris. "Isn't it bad enough that we've lost the best canine companion in the world without you making up silly stories?"

"What's a canine companion?" asked Benjy.

"A dog, idiot," said Kayla.

Why couldn't Mrs Harris have just said dog then? It was typical of her to use two big words when one small one would do.

Benjy could still see Jonah. He was sitting quietly by the cheese plant, licking one of his paws.

"Can't you see him?" said Benjy, still very much afraid.

"You're a very cruel boy, making things up at a time like this," said Mrs Harris.

"Our dog's dead, and you killed him," added Kayla, and not for the first time. "He won't ever come back again because of you. It's all your fault!"

"I'm very disappointed in you, Benjy," said his father, and they all went back upstairs, shaking their heads over Benjy's terrible behaviour.

"It's not fair," Benjy muttered to himself. He wasn't feeling very well, so he sat on a chair at the kitchen table.

Jonah looked at him as if to say, "I'll tell you what isn't fair, it's being cut down in your prime."

"I didn't do it on purpose," Benjy said. "It just happened. It was an accident waiting to happen." Jonah got up and walked over to Benjy's chair. Benjy looked at him. "It was an accident waiting to happen," he repeated. His mother always used to say that to him when he'd dropped something or bumped his head on the corner of the table. "You can't blame me for it. You just kept running. I tried to warn you but you didn't listen." Benjy's mother used to say that to him too.

Jonah looked at Benjy as if to say, "Oh, I blame you all right. You should have been more careful. I was too young to die."

Benjy sighed. "It wasn't my fault," he repeated.

Jonah said nothing, but the look on his face meant, "It's never your fault, is it?"

"Don't you start as well," said Benjy. "That's all I hear, morning, noon and night."

Jonah put his two front paws on Benjy's leg as if to say, "Maybe you should listen then."

"Look, if I needed a lecture from a canine companion, I would ask for one, OK?"

Jonah's shaggy brown eyebrows went up as if he was saying, "Like you have a choice. What are you going to do? Send me over another cliff?"

"IT WAS AN ACCIDENT!"

And if Jonah had been alive and able to talk he would have said, "Yeah, yeah, but it's no excuse."

That night, Benjy lay in bed, staring at the ceiling. He was too worried to sleep. He used to put all his imagination into thinking about City. He used to fantasize about being their top scorer. Now his imagination had gone into overdrive, but he no longer thought about nice, exciting things. No, he thought about small brown dogs and saw them running around the house when nobody else could see them.

Benjy sat up and turned on the light again. He thought he saw Jonah standing by the door, but when he blinked there was nothing there. What was going on? He rubbed his eyes. Perhaps the problem wasn't his brain. Perhaps it was his eyes. Maybe he just needed glasses. Benjy snuggled down into the duvet with the City cover. Yes, that was it. His eyes were playing tricks on him. He made up his mind to ask his dad about an eye test first thing the next morning.

seven

Benjy was in the bathroom. His dad was busy and Benjy was taking the opportunity to do some serious sailing. His dad said it was a waste of water, and he wouldn't let him do it but, since he wasn't there, Benjy was really enjoying filling the bath, rolling up his sleeves and pushing his boats up and down slowly. It helped him to think. Jonah was sitting quietly beside him.

"Get lost," Benjy told him repeatedly as he pushed his yellow steamboat and watched it float towards the taps.

Jonah didn't move. He seemed to enjoy winding Benjy up. "You don't get rid of me that easily, Dog Killer," he seemed to be saying.

"It was an accident," said Benjy, as usual.

Jonah just looked at him.

"I'm sorry, OK?"

It was obvious that Jonah didn't believe him. He cocked his head on one side and looked at Benjy accusingly.

Benjy tried to ignore him. He got out his big blue boat, his absolute favourite, adjusted its sails and lowered it into the water.

There was a rap at the door. "Let me in, Benjy, I really need to go. You've been in there for ages and ages. It's not fair!"

It was Kayla. She was banging on the door and making a nuisance of herself. Didn't she understand that Benjy needed peace and quiet? What with Kayla and Mrs Harris (not to mention the ghost of the dog), everything was busy and complicated all the time. It had never been like this before *they* had moved in. Benjy wished it could go back to being just him and Dad.

Mrs Harris's voice boomed out, "It's time you were finished, Benjy. What do you think you're doing? You've been in there for more than half an hour!"

"It's private," Benjy answered. "Leave me alone!"

"You've got to learn to think about other people, not just yourself. It isn't fair to hog the bathroom. Just open the door."

Benjy sighed. He lifted out his boats and dried them carefully on one of the towels. But before he could pull the plug out of the bath, Jonah stood up and leaped into the water, sending a shower up the walls and leaving huge puddles on the floor. "Get out!" Benjy yelled and tried to heave Jonah from the water, but he simply continued to splash, drenching Benjy in the process. Then, just as suddenly as he'd dived in, Jonah jumped out again, shaking himself dry and sending more spray everywhere.

Benjy grabbed all the towels from the rails and tried to mop up the water. "You idiot!" he hissed at Jonah, but the dog had vanished again.

"Open that door now!" Mrs Harris shouted. Her voice sounded even fiercer than it did at school. Benjy opened the door slowly.

Mrs Harris took a sharp breath when she

saw the mess. "What on earth have you been doing?" she said.

"Sailing my boats," said Benjy. "Dad always lets me," he fibbed.

Mrs Harris picked up a sopping towel. "Look at this," she said. Then she pointed to the walls. "And this! What on earth possessed you to make such a mess?"

"It wasn't me," said Benjy.

"No, it never is you, is it?" answered Mrs Harris. "Why can't you just own up to things?"

"It wasn't me," Benjy repeated. He was almost crying.

"Well it wasn't me," said Mrs Harris, "and it certainly wasn't your father. And it can't have been Kayla because she's been downstairs with me. So that just leaves you."

"And the dog," said Benjy.

Mrs Harris stepped towards Benjy and looked at him as if he was the meanest boy who had ever lived. "Every time we try to talk to you about your behaviour, you bring up that dog. Isn't it enough that he's gone because of you? Why do you have to make things worse all the time?"

"I'm not," said Benjy softly. It wasn't fair. Why wouldn't anyone believe him? That rotten dog was really making him pay for what happened on that cliff. He'd probably have to suffer for the rest of his life, always getting the blame for things that weren't his fault. Benjy glared at Mrs Harris. He wasn't going to cry. He was absolutely determined not to give her the satisfaction.

"Right. Well, you can clear all this up. Go downstairs to the kitchen and fetch a mop and bucket. I want to see everything tidy and dry in the next half-hour. And don't think you'll be watching any television this evening. I'll be speaking to your father."

Benjy trudged downstairs. Jonah was at his heels again. "Look, just go away," Benjy said. "Haven't you done enough? Dad will go ape about that mess when she tells him. It's *so* not fair." Benjy dragged the mop out of the cupboard. Jonah sniffed the bucket and rubbed his back against the vacuum cleaner, sending it crashing to the floor. "Careful!" said Benjy. "She'll blame me for that as well in a minute."

He was being dogged, haunted, reduced to a shivering wreck by this animal. His life was a total nightmare.

It took him an hour to clean everything up. Jonah just watched. "You could pick up a cloth and help a bit," said Benjy. "After all, it was you."

Jonah wagged his tail.

"Talking to yourself again?" said Kayla, sneaking up behind him. "You know what that's a sign of, don't you? Being a dog killer has turned your brain. I bet you've gone mad with guilt. Mum says it happens to people all the time. They feel so bad about the things they've done that they flip, just like that."

"Don't be stupid," Benjy said.

"We should make you pay a fine every time you use the word stupid. We'd make a fortune," said Kayla.

"Well, you are *stupid*. I can't help it if it's the word that suits you best."

"You can't call me stupid because you're mad, so what you think doesn't count."

"Well, if I am going mad it's because you and

your mum have pushed me into it," said Benjy.

"As if you needed any help from us," Kayla replied. "Still seeing things?"

"No."

"What about that dog sitting beside you?"

"You can see it too?" said Benjy, full of relief. Now, at last, they'd have to believe him.

"Got you there," said Kayla. "Did you think I really meant it?"

Benjy looked at her. It was clear from her face that she didn't really think that Jonah was there. Benjy felt terribly disappointed. "Go away," he said miserably. "Just leave me alone."

"'Leave me alone, leave me alone', that's all you ever say. Apart from 'it's not my fault' or 'it's not fair' or 'don't be stupid', of course."

Benjy bit his lip. Well, it wasn't fair. It wasn't. He continued to mop the floor in silence while Jonah sat and watched. If only Kayla and Mrs Harris had never come to live with them, everything would have been all right.

Benjy thought of his mum then. She was in Ohio, which was somewhere in America. His dad had shown him on the map. It was hundreds and hundreds of miles away. If only she was still around. She would have understood about the dog. Benjy kicked the bucket angrily. Jonah growled. Benjy couldn't believe it. Just his luck to be haunted by the ghost of his wicked step-mother's dog.

eight

"You need glasses, young man," the optician said.

It was his eyes then. Benjy was so relieved that he forgot to worry about being teased in the playground by Paul Fish and being called Four Eyes.

"Will they stop me seeing things?" he asked.

"Don't be silly," answered his dad. He didn't understand what Benjy meant. "They'll help you to see more clearly," he added.

Benjy went to choose some frames. There were blue ones and brown ones and orange ones. He picked up the nearest pair and tried them on. "These are OK," he said.

"No, Benjy, take some time over it. You

always rush things. You need to choose the pair that suits you best."

Benjy was bored already but he tried to be patient. He let his dad pick out half a dozen pairs, which he tried on dutifully.

"The small brown ones, I think," said Andy, staring at him hard. "Look in the mirror, Ben."

Benjy looked. He didn't seem the same at all with glasses on. It was rather worrying. So many things were changing lately and now he looked different on top of everything else.

Benjy took the glasses off and placed them in his father's hand. "OK," he said. If glasses prevented Jonah from turning up again, the change in his appearance would be worth it.

"It will take about two weeks to get these made up," the optician said as they went to pay.

"Two weeks? Can't I have them now?"

"We like to do a proper job making up our glasses, not like some opticians you go to these days. Proper jobs take time," the optician replied.

"Benjy's always in a hurry for things," his father explained. "You know what kids are like."

The optician nodded. He said he had three of his own.

Benjy thought he might cry for a moment. He was glad that Kayla and Mrs Harris had gone off to do some shopping of their own. He was tired of being told off or laughed at and they would have laughed like anything to see him being so pathetic.

"What's the matter, Benjy?" his father asked.

"Nothing," he answered.

They left the optician's and walked along the high street. Suddenly, Jonah had joined them. He was bouncing along behind Benjy as if everything was the way it had been before the cliff happened. Benjy mouthed at him to go away and kicked a can hard across the pavement. It almost hit Jonah, who had to swerve to avoid it.

"It isn't fair," Benjy muttered.

"What isn't fair, Benjy?" asked his dad. "If we go to the burger place, will you tell me what's wrong? You haven't been yourself since the accident with the dog."

"OK," said Benjy, cheering up a little.

They sat at a corner table by the window.

Jonah curled himself up under Benjy's chair.

"So what's the matter?" said his father.

"Everybody blames me for everything," Benjy answered. "It wasn't my fault about Jonah."

"Let's forget about all that now. It was a real shame but I know you didn't do it on purpose. I'm not cross any more."

"Aren't you? What about Mrs Harris and Kayla?"

"Carol's all right about it. She knows it was an accident too. Kayla misses Jonah a lot and because she's young she may not let it go so easily. You'll just have to ignore her until she gets over it. I thought I might get her a fish tank and some goldfish to take her mind off it."

"I don't like goldfish." Steven had fish and they were dead boring. They just swam about doing nothing. And it took hours to clean out the tank. Benjy could picture Mrs Harris making him do it on Saturday mornings when he wanted to play football or something. "I don't want us to get fish, I don't like fish," Benjy repeated.

"You don't like anything much, Benjy, that's your problem. You'll have to like it or lump it this time. We have to think about doing something nice for Kayla."

What about me? thought Benjy. He kept his mouth shut though. He didn't want any more trouble.

Benjy opened the box that contained his Kid's Meal. It was a bit babyish but he still liked them. His mother had always bought them for him, before she'd gone to America. "Do you want some of my shake?" he asked his dad.

Andy shook his head. "I might get myself a coffee in a minute."

Benjy unwrapped his toy. It was a blue donkey with legs that moved. "I've already got this," he said.

"Shall I see if we can swap it?"

Benjy shook his head. "I've got the whole set now. I thought they'd be on to a different set this week."

"Never mind," said his father, relieved that Benjy was being calm about his disappointment for once. "You know, you can be really sensible sometimes, Ben."

"I am a good boy really," Benjy said.

"I know you are." His dad took his hand and said, "I'm sorry I didn't tell you about Carol and Kayla sooner. It would probably have made it easier for you. I took the line of least resistance and it's caused a lot of trouble."

"What's the line of least resistance?"

"It means I took the easy way of doing things. We're not that different, you and me."

Benjy smiled. He liked the idea that he was the same as his dad. He felt happy and warm, and the bad feelings of the last few weeks began to disappear.

Just as Benjy was thinking that life really wasn't so bad after all, Kayla and Mrs Harris came bounding up to them.

"Where did you two spring from?" Andy said.

"We were next door getting some jeans," said Carol. "Kayla saw you come in so we decided to join you. I'm starving."

"Can I have a Kid's Meal too?" asked Kayla, looking at Benjy's box.

"Go on," said Carol, giving her some money. "And get me a quarter pounder and a large fries."

Benjy went quiet. Why did they always have

to spoil everything? He was having one of the best days ever with his dad and now he had to share it.

"Benjy does need glasses," Andy told Carol.

"I thought you might. You're always peering at the board."

"It's nothing to do with her," Benjy told his dad.

"Don't be rude, Ben," his father replied.

Kayla returned then with a trayful of food.

"Where's my ketchup?" Mrs Harris said.

Benjy stared at her as she dipped her fries in the ketchup two at a time and stuffed them into her mouth. She was never like this at school. It was as if she was two different people sometimes. Benjy felt topsy-turvy again.

"When can we go home?" he said.

"We've only just got here. You asked to come. I thought you liked this place," said his father.

Benjy shrugged. He got up and went over to the noticeboard. He wanted to be by himself. There were ads for jobs and things for sale. Someone was getting rid of a computer with hundreds of games. And there was a bike for under twenty quid. He'd always wanted a bike and that was a real bargain.

Benjy went back to the table. "Dad—" he said.

"Whatever it is, you can't have it."

"You don't even know what I was going to say," said Benjy.

"I've got a good idea. You always want something when you've looked at that noticeboard."

Benjy threw himself into his seat. The table rocked.

"Careful, Benjy," Mrs Harris said.

Kayla pulled a face at him.

"I want to go home," Benjy repeated.

But his dad wasn't listening. He had his hand on top of Mrs Harris's and they were speaking in low voices. Every now and then, they giggled like a couple of kids. It was so embarrassing that Benjy hardly knew where to look.

Two weeks later, Benjy's glasses were ready for collection. Jonah was sitting beside the woman who was about to check that they fitted properly. Benjy put them on and suddenly everything became much clearer. "I can see," he said. "See properly, I mean."

"I should have realized you needed glasses," his dad replied. "I'm sorry, Ben."

Benjy looked towards Jonah, expecting him to have faded to nothing now that his eyesight was working normally, but Jonah was still visible – even more clearly than before.

"I don't believe this!" Benjy said.

"What is it?" asked his dad.

"Nothing," Benjy replied. He'd been so sure that Jonah would go once his eye problems were sorted out. He couldn't believe that the dog was still there.

All the way home, Benjy could almost hear Jonah chanting "Four Eyes". He was certainly smiling at Benjy's bad luck.

He was stuck with wearing glasses and, if that wasn't bad enough, he was still being haunted by a dog. Benjy put his head in his hands. It was hard to see how his life could get any worse.

nine

"Benjy! I'm leaving in one minute and I'm not going to be made late by you. Get a move on!"

Mrs Harris's voice boomed up the staircase. Benjy grabbed his jacket and backpack and hurried down. He followed Mrs Harris out to the car. Kayla was already waiting beside it.

"When will you learn to be on time, Benjy?" Mrs Harris said. "Kayla's been ready for the last ten minutes. I seem to spend half my life waiting for you."

"Nobody asked you to," Benjy muttered. "Anyway, Dad's a lot worse than me and you don't care at all when he's late."

"That's where you're wrong, but your dad doesn't make me late for work. You do."

"What does being late matter?"

"If you're late you keep people waiting. They can't do the things they need to do and everybody gets held up."

"People should just learn to chill."

"*What?*"

"Nothing," answered Benjy crossly. As Mrs Harris started the car, Benjy gave Kayla a little pinch for looking so pleased with herself.

"Ow," she said. "Mum, Benjy pinched me."

"Telltale," said Benjy. "Sneak. Rotten grass."

"Be quiet, you two," said Mrs Harris.

"That's not fair!" said Kayla. "He started it."

"I don't care who started it. Just behave, the pair of you."

It was going to be one of those days, thought Benjy as he caught sight of Jonah. He was snuggling into the back seat next to Kayla, who didn't even know he was there. Benjy wondered what mischief he might get up to. Was he intending to come into Benjy's class or would he stay in the car?

Benjy soon found out. As soon as Mrs Harris had parked in her usual space, Jonah bounded out and followed Benjy across the playground. "Go away," he said. "Stop following me, you stupid mutt, I'm not in the mood."

Jonah just looked at him as if he didn't care what mood Benjy was in. Benjy decided to ignore him. That was what his dad always said. "If someone's bothering you, Benjy, just walk away from them. Pretend they're not even there. Otherwise, you just get into trouble."

Benjy seldom followed his dad's advice, but that particular morning it seemed a good idea. Benjy decided not to speak to Jonah any more. He wouldn't even look at him. That way, the dog might get the message and disappear again.

But Jonah remained stubbornly beside Benjy. When he sat at his usual table, Jonah curled up underneath it, next to Benjy's foot. It felt strange to have a dog in the classroom that no one else could see. Benjy wanted to tell someone what was happening but he knew no one would believe him. They would just think he was telling lies or being silly. He almost felt like bursting with the secret. He wanted to turn to Steven and say, "There's a dog right here. I can see him just as clearly as I can see you, but he's invisible to everybody else. He's a ghost dog." Even as Benjy repeated the words to himself, he could tell how silly they sounded. Everyone would think he was crazy. They'd laugh at him for being such a nutcase.

Mrs Harris spoke to the class. "All right, everyone, I'm going to collect your homework."

Everybody rustled in their bags for their workbooks. Benjy groped for his but he couldn't find it. He lifted his backpack onto his knee and searched again. It wasn't there. He never used to bother with homework, but now that he lived with Mrs Harris he didn't really have a choice. She went on and on at him all the time. "Have you done that arithmetic I gave you yesterday? And what about that story I told you to write?" So last night he'd spent ages on his spelling and made his writing the neatest it had ever been. He couldn't believe that he'd forgotten to pack it. He could actually remember putting it in the bag, but if he had, it would have been there, wouldn't it?

And then a terrible thought struck him. He

peered under the table and looked at Jonah. There were little scraps of paper strewn around the floor and tatters hanging from Jonah's mouth. The rotten mutt looked really pleased with himself. He was practically smiling.

"I don't believe this!" said Benjy out loud.

"Benjy Dobson, stop talking to yourself and give me your homework."

"I haven't got it."

At that moment, there was a knock at the door. Benjy sighed with relief. With luck, it would distract Mrs Harris, take her attention away from him. It was Paul Fish with a message from the head teacher.

"Just wait there a minute, Paul," said Mrs Harris, gesturing to the space beside her desk. "I'm dealing with something."

Benjy groaned inside. Not only was he about to be humiliated in front of the whole class but Paul Fish was going to get a ringside seat. Mrs Harris turned back to Benjy and, as if there had been no interruption, she said, "Last night, you told me you'd finished all your homework. I let you watch television because of it."

"I did do it. It just isn't here."

"Did you forget to put it in your bag?"

Benjy nodded. There was no point in trying to tell her the truth. She'd never believe him.

Mrs Harris walked over to Benjy's table. She bent down and picked up a torn piece of paper. "What's this?" she said.

Benjy gave in. "I think it's a bit of paper from my workbook."

"How did it get torn? And why is it on the floor?" Mrs Harris peered under the table. She gathered up a whole pile of torn pages with Benjy's writing on them. "What on earth have you been doing?"

"It wasn't me. I mean, it wasn't my fault. I didn't do it."

"Are you telling me that somebody else did this?"

Benjy nodded.

"Somebody else here in this classroom?"

Benjy nodded again.

"Who was it?" Mrs Harris boomed. "Who did this?"

The whole class went quiet.

"It wasn't another person," Benjy said at last.

"So who was it? The bogeyman?"

"Sort of," Benjy said.

Everybody laughed, especially Paul Fish, who had to hold on to the edge of Mrs Harris's desk to stop himself keeling over with the sheer excitement of it. His eyes started to water. He even got hiccups. Steven laughed too, but every now and then he stopped and gave Benjy a sympathetic look.

That made Benjy crosser than ever. He didn't want sympathy and he especially didn't want it from Steven. He wanted Steven to look up to him and think he was cool. He didn't want him thinking he was a silly little kid who made up crazy stories.

Everyone stopped laughing eventually. Mrs Harris said, "Well, I've heard some excuses in my time but this takes some beating. If you're going to tell stories, at least make them believable. You can stay in at break. I won't have things destroyed in my classroom. Do you know how much paper costs? Think about the trees. Thousands of trees get cut down every year to make paper. When you waste paper, you waste trees. You destroy them."

Benjy sighed. As if it wasn't enough to be a dog killer, he had turned into a tree killer as well in Mrs Harris's eyes.

"Now then, Paul, I believe you have a message for me," Mrs Harris said.

Paul repeated some stuff about a PTA meeting. He walked past Benjy's table on the way out, paused and said, "Nutter," under his breath. Benjy flushed and decided that the day could only get better.

But it didn't. At break, when he was kept in, he got a whole lot of talk from Mrs Harris about his bad behaviour. She went on and on. "You could be such a nice boy, Benjy, but you don't even try most of the time. And why did you destroy your homework? What was that about? Is something troubling you? Is this about how upset you're feeling about all the changes at home? I'm here to help, Benjy. I don't want us to be fighting all the time, it isn't good for either of us."

"You've got that right."

"Benjy, I'm trying to be patient here. Why don't you start trying too? You make no effort to meet people halfway. All I want is some kind of explanation."

"I don't have an explanation, or not one that you'd believe. You'd just say I was making it up."

"Try me."

"There isn't any point. You won't believe me."

"Try, Benjy. I might surprise you."

"OK, then. Jonah's here. He ate my homework."

Mrs Harris did surprise Benjy. She started to laugh. "The 'dog ate my homework' excuse. At least you've given it a twist. At least it's the ghost of a dog."

"It isn't funny," said Benjy angrily. He hated being laughed at.

"Listen, I know you're upset about a lot of things at the moment, so I'm not going to say any more about this. But please, Benjy, try to think before you do silly things. Tearing up your homework out of some kind of anger just doesn't solve a thing, and it's very foolish to make up stories to cover up the things you've done. People see through them."

Benjy gave up. He'd known all along. There was no point in explaining. She hadn't believed him. Still, at least she hadn't punished him any more either.

That evening, after tea, when Benjy's dad came home late from work, Mrs Harris said to him, "Wait till you hear Benjy's latest excuse for not handing in his story." And she told him all about the ghost dog who supposedly ate Benjy's homework. Benjy felt a complete idiot. He wished that the crew of the space ship Enterprise would beam him up and take him off the planet. He felt himself blushing again as his dad burst out laughing.

"But it *is* true," Benjy said.

Everyone laughed some more, especially Kayla. And the worst thing was, when Benjy looked at the floor he could see Jonah, and Jonah was laughing too.

ten

First thing on Sunday morning, a wonderful idea occurred to Benjy. He'd seen this film once called *Ghostbusters*. There were people in it who got rid of ghosts. They squirted them with stuff and watched them melt away. It was the best.

There were bound to be some ghostbusters in Manchester, it was just a question of finding them. He remembered that, when his dad had wanted a plumber the other day, he'd looked one up in *Yellow Pages*. Benjy pulled out a chair and stood on it to reach the phone books. Jonah got up and stood beside him, wagging his tail so hard against the chair that it began to wobble. "Go away!" Benjy shouted, but

Jonah just carried on wagging. Benjy squealed as the chair he was standing on crashed to the floor.

Everyone came running downstairs. His dad began to help him up but Mrs Harris said, "No, leave him there, he might have broken something."

For a minute, Benjy thought Mrs Harris meant that he ought to be left lying on the floor if he'd broken anything valuable, as a kind of punishment. Then he realized she was talking about broken bones and was worried that he might have hurt himself. "Lie still, Benjy," she said.

"What on earth were you doing, Ben?" asked his dad.

"Trying to get something off the shelf. The chair just tipped." There was no point in trying to explain about Jonah. Nobody believed him anyway.

"Can you move your leg?" said Mrs Harris. It hurt a bit, but Benjy managed to lift it slightly, and to waggle his toes. "What about your arm?" Benjy tried to move it and a sharp pain went through him. He yelled again, and imagined that being shot with a bow and arrow felt a bit like that.

Mrs Harris turned to Andy. "I think his arm might be broken. He needs to go to A & E for an X-ray."

"I've got to go into work. They've just rung me. I'm on call this weekend, remember?"

"Don't worry, I'll take him. He'll be fine."

"I want Dad to do it," Benjy said.

"I can't, Ben."

"If she didn't live with us, you'd have to. You wouldn't have any choice."

"Well, Carol does live with us, Benjy, and I'm very glad of it. Come on, go and get your coat. You too, Kayla," said Andy.

"United's playing. You promised you'd take me, Mum," Kayla complained.

"Sorry, Kayla, this comes first."

"It's not fair," said Benjy and Kayla, at exactly the same time.

"Just get your coats," answered Carol and Andy together.

* * *

As they drove to the hospital, Benjy wished with all his heart that Jonah could be seen by other people, not just him. The nervous break-down he'd been thinking about had probably happened on the day his dad married Mrs Harris, and seeing Jonah was a sign of it. Mrs Jenkins said that you went all funny when you had a break-down. Benjy felt very funny indeed most of the time.

"Is it still hurting, Benjy?" asked Kayla. She sounded quite kind.

Benjy nodded. It was hurting so much that he felt like crying.

As if she knew what he was thinking, Mrs Harris said, "You're being very brave, Benjy."

Praise from Mrs Harris! It was like a miracle.

Kayla held Benjy's good arm and stroked it gently, the way she used to stroke Jonah. Benjy felt warm and happy for a moment and then remembered that he didn't like her, or her horrible Big Foot mother. They were living in his house and turning his dad into a complete stranger, someone he didn't even know any more. He pulled away from Kayla.

They had a long wait at the hospital. Loads and loads of people got seen before they did. There was a man with blood all over his trouser leg. It made Benjy feel sick, but Kayla couldn't take her eyes off him.

"I bet he had an accident and cut himself. I bet it's really deep. He probably needs a blood transfusion like vampires do. I could give blood," she said.

There was a boy, two or three years older than they were, with a bandaged head. "Concussion," said Kayla at once. "I've seen it on television. They'll be banging on his chest in a minute and sticking tubes down his throat."

"They only do that to unconscious people," said Benjy.

"He'll be unconscious in a minute, I bet you anything," Kayla replied.

"I bet you chips at McDonald's that he won't," said Benjy.

"You're on," said Kayla.

But before anything could happen one way or another, the boy was taken off to a curtained cubicle by one of the nurses.

"He'll have passed out by now," said Kayla after a few minutes.

"No he won't, he was fine."

"Then why did that nurse take him away?"

"Well, not *fine* then, but he's not unconscious, I'm sure he isn't."

"I win the bet," said Kayla.

"No you don't, the bet's off, you've got to have proof."

"I'll go and ask then."

"As if I'd take your word," said Benjy.

"Mum, will you ask?" Kayla said.

"Ask what?" Mrs Harris replied, looking up from the magazine she'd been reading.

"Ask about the boy who just got taken away by the nurse. We want to know whether he's passed out yet."

"Don't be so silly."

"We want to know," said Kayla again.

"Why? What's it to you?"

"We just want to know, that's all," said Kayla, kicking the seat in front of her.

"It's none of your business. Now just sit still and wait quietly."

"The bet's off," said Benjy again.

"That's not fair, I would have won."

"The bet's off. If you can't get proof, you can't win."

"Well, you didn't win either."

"Be quiet, you two," said Mrs Harris, looking up from her magazine once more. "If I have to tell you again, there'll be trouble."

Benjy's arm was broken. He had to have an X-ray to prove it and then they put it in a plaster cast. Kayla was beside herself with envy. "Can I write on it?" she said.

"If you have to," Benjy answered, though secretly he was pleased. Joseph Edwards had got a plaster cast last year through jumping off a five-foot wall and people had given him sweets and made a great fuss of him.

"Can I have some chocolate?" asked Benjy when it was all over.

"Go on then. Kayla, go and get a couple of bars out of that machine."

Benjy smiled to himself. "What about my homework?" he asked Mrs Harris as Kayla went to get the chocolate. "I won't be able to do my reading now."

"Don't be silly, Benjy, you don't read with your arms."

"I won't be able to turn the pages."

"I'm sure you'll manage somehow."

Benjy felt gloomy again for a moment, but then another thought struck him. "I won't be able to write properly though, will I? Not with my writing arm in plaster."

Mrs Harris had to admit he had a point. As Benjy chewed the chocolate Kayla had brought him, he thought that things could have been a whole lot worse.

In the car, on the way home, Kayla held Benjy's good arm again and patted it gently. He was aching badly, so this time he didn't stop her doing it, he just put up with it and told himself that it didn't make any difference – he still hated her.

Jonah was asleep on the car floor, just by Benjy's feet. He was snoring. Benjy prodded him with his foot as a punishment for causing his broken arm. But Jonah didn't stir, he just kept snoozing. And even in his sleep he looked pleased with himself, as if he was happy to be causing Benjy so much aggravation.

eleven

It was going to be the match of the season. Benjy had been looking forward to it from the moment he'd seen the fixture list. United versus City on United's turf. Benjy was desperate to watch his team thrash United, mash them to pieces, utterly destroy every bit of them. Sometimes, he even dreamed about it. "United's going to win," Kayla kept saying, just to wind him up.

She said it again at breakfast that morning. Benjy banged his fist on the table, causing the cereal packet to jump. Jonah growled from under Benjy's chair, making him calm down a little. You could never be sure what a ghost dog might do next and Benjy had a feeling that Jonah's teeth were even sharper now than they used to be.

So Benjy just told Kayla to shut up, rather more quietly than he might have done.

"United's bound to win," said Kayla. She just couldn't stop herself. "City are a bunch of losers."

"Be quiet, Kayla," Mrs Harris said without glancing up from the newspaper she was reading.

"My dad says it's rude to read at the table," said Benjy.

Mrs Harris glared at him for a moment. Then she put the newspaper to one side and said, "Sorry, it's an old habit. Your dad's right, it is rude." She smiled at Andy who was standing by the sink and he smiled back at her.

Benjy was taken by surprise. She'd given in just like that. She was even being nice. He realized later that he should have known she had something up her sleeve, something that would practically ruin his entire life forever.

And then she said it: "I got tickets for the match last night. I had to queue for hours."

"Brilliant!" said Andy and Kayla together.

"They were really hard to get. I didn't think we'd be lucky but they let me have the four I asked for."

Andy came over and gave her a kiss. Benjy nearly puked.

"Say thank you to Carol then," said Andy, looking at Benjy.

"Thanks," said Benjy automatically.

"We'll all be sitting together," Mrs Harris said. "It'll be a fantastic day out."

Sitting together? thought Benjy. That was silly. Kayla and Mrs Harris would be with the United crowd and he and his dad would be at the City end, with the other away supporters. He started to say as much.

"No, Ben," said Andy. "I couldn't get the tickets myself, I didn't have time, and Carol could only get United seats at their end of the stadium. But it will be nice for us to go as a family and sit with each other."

"But we'll be at the wrong end. I won't be able to wear my hat or scarf or the United lot will mash me to pieces. And we'll be cheering for City on our own. The United supporters will drown us out. Don't you see, Dad? It just won't work."

"It's a done deal, Benjy. We can leave our

scarves at home for once. What does it matter? It's only a game."

Only a game? Benjy knew that his dad would never have said such a thing before he met Mrs Harris. She'd changed him completely. He wasn't even the same person any more. Benjy tried again. "Dad, come on. It's the best match of the season. We've got to do it properly or it won't be worth going."

"Don't be silly, Benjy," said his dad.

"I don't see what the fuss is about," said Mrs Harris. "You'll still see your team. The view's the same whether you're at one end or the other."

Benjy banged his fist on the table again, in the hope that this would get through to them. He just couldn't believe how stupid they were being. Jonah growled again, more loudly than before.

"Enough, Benjy," said Andy in his angriest voice.

"It's not fair!"

"You're going to the match. Carol's gone to a lot of trouble to get those tickets. The least you can do is be grateful."

"But I'm not grateful. Why should I be grateful? The whole day's ruined and it's all her fault!"

Benjy ran out of the room and went upstairs. He leaned against his bedroom door to stop anyone from coming after him. It was no good though. Mrs Harris forced her way in, using her big feet to push the door open. Jonah followed.

Benjy sat on the floor, trying not to show how scared he was. Mrs Harris looked blazing mad and Jonah was growling. Benjy began to think that it would be better to face a cage full of hungry lions than to deal with the two of them. "Sorry," he murmured. Anything to get the pair of them off his back.

"I should think so," Mrs Harris said. "What's got into you, Benjy? You used to be such a nice little boy."

Benjy could hardly believe his ears. Mrs Harris had always hated him, right from the moment they'd first set eyes on one another. How could she pretend that she'd ever thought he was nice?

"I know it isn't easy for you, having a stepmother and getting used to sharing things with Kayla, but I'm trying really hard to do the right thing by you. It's time you started doing the right thing by me."

"OK," said Benjy, just to shut her up.

"I'd like an apology, please."

It seemed to Benjy that this was taking things too far. He really, really hated saying sorry, and it wasn't like he'd even mean it. He just sat in silence. Jonah growled so loudly that Benjy jumped.

Mrs Harris took his arm. "Hey, what's the matter?" she said in a softer voice. "You're really jumpy today. Calm down, come on. Deep breaths. Think of City winning that game. You want to see the match, don't you? Will it really be so bad to sit on the other side of the stadium? You'll see everything, I promise, and we'll have a really good day with nice things to eat, and maybe go to a film or something in the evening."

Benjy was expecting her to say that she was still waiting for him to say sorry, but instead she got up to go.

For a moment, Benjy thought he could apologize, but nothing seemed to happen. He thought the word *sorry* over and over in his head, but he couldn't make it come out of his mouth. There was just silence. As Mrs Harris went downstairs again, Benjy wished things weren't so muddled up. He'd almost liked her for a moment and it seemed as if his brain would explode with the confusion of it.

twelve

Benjy's hands felt freezing as he sat waiting for the match to start. He blew on them every now and then to warm them a little.

"I told you to remember your gloves, Benjy," Mrs Harris said. She was such a know-it-all.

Kayla nudged him. "Do you want to wear mine for a bit?" she said.

Benjy could see that this was a nice gesture but he was too fed up to appreciate it. Besides, Kayla's gloves were pink with silver stars on them – he'd look a complete girl in them. So he just shook his head and pulled a face at her.

His dad silently took off his jacket and wrapped it round Benjy's shoulders.

"You'll be cold now."

"No I won't," said Andy. "Anyway, it's only for a few minutes, while you warm up."

Benjy spread the hem of the jacket over his knees. He was starting to feel warmer already. Carol produced a City fanzine. Benjy took it without a word but no one mentioned that he should say thank you. He wondered why everyone was being so nice to him. Perhaps it was because his arm was still in plaster and he was wearing a sling. Even complete strangers were giving him sympathetic smiles. It was utterly depressing, having kindness when you were in a bad mood. What he wanted was a nice fat row with someone, a chance to shout and cry for a while. They were getting it all wrong.

The players came out onto the pitch and a few minutes later the match began. Why couldn't they have been sitting at the City end? Benjy thought. It would be so much better. He looked down for a moment, expecting to see Jonah sitting under the seat, or trying to eat the rest of the sandwiches in his dad's bag, but he'd disappeared.

Benjy turned his attention back to the match. Even in the first five minutes, it became clear that

City could actually win. They were playing really well and keeping possession of the ball – they'd already managed a couple of near misses. Benjy began to forget he was at the wrong end of the pitch. The game was so exciting he could hardly sit still. He imagined the glory of having his team win and rubbing Kayla's nose in her side's defeat. He started to feel puffed up with happiness.

And then, as if the very thought had jinxed City's chances of victory, it all began to go wrong. The players started to stumble about and to miss easy kicks like a bunch of amateurs. Benjy watched in disbelief as one after another they tripped up or sent the ball in totally the wrong direction. And then the problem became clear. Jonah slowly began to appear: first his tail, then his body, and then his legs became visible to Benjy. And he was darting all over the pitch, butting the ball with the weight of his whole body so that it swerved away from the City players every time they went anywhere near it.

"The wind's really bad today," said Andy, "it keeps blowing the ball towards United's goal."

"It isn't the wind," said Benjy, but his words

were lost in the cheers of the United supporters as their team scored.

Kayla and Mrs Harris jumped up and started waving in the air. It was so mean of them, Benjy thought, to be so pleased about City's misfortune. He covered his face with his good hand, unable to believe what Jonah was doing. How could he be so stupid? He was ruining City's chances of a win. Benjy looked at the pitch again and saw Jonah nudging the ball away from City's best striker.

"NO!" Benjy shouted, but Jonah ignored him completely and rolled the ball as fast as he could towards United's goal again. Within seconds, United had goal number two. "I don't believe it!" Benjy shouted. "Dad, did you see that?"

"Never mind, City can still equalize. There's plenty of time."

"Two goals down in the first ten minutes. Jonah's doing this on purpose."

"What are you talking about, Ben?"

"Can't you see what he's doing?"

"What do you mean? I can't see anything. It's just the wind."

"Here, Jonah, come back here," Benjy shouted but, again, his cries were drowned in the roar of the crowd. "He's ignoring me!"

"Do you want some more orange juice?" Mrs Harris asked, as if nothing unusual was happening.

"Can you see what he's doing?" Benjy asked.

"What do you mean? Who's doing what?"

"Never mind," Benjy said, and he fell silent again. What was the point? No one else could see Jonah, so how could they believe him? Jonah had thought of the perfect punishment for Benjy by destroying City's chances of winning the match. The dog wasn't as stupid as he looked.

Jonah came bounding back as the final whistle blew. He was wagging his tail and looking pleased with himself.

"You rotten dog!" Benjy said. "How could you do that? You ruined everything."

Jonah just wagged his tail even more. It was obviously what he'd intended all along.

City lost by fifteen goals to nil. It was bad enough to get them into the *Guinness Book of Records*. All the City supporters hung their heads in shame. There was nothing you could say when your team lost that badly. You just had to try to get over it.

Benjy was silent on the way home in the car. He felt the defeat very deeply, especially as he knew that he was to blame; if Jonah hadn't gone over that cliff, he wouldn't have been looking for revenge.

"I'm sorry, Dad," said Benjy.

"What for?"

"City losing."

"It wasn't your fault, Ben. Cheer up, there's always Arsenal next Saturday."

Benjy did cheer up a little then. It was an away game, so Jonah wouldn't be able to mess it up.

Kayla sang United victory songs all the way home. Mrs Harris told her to shut up but she wouldn't. Benjy put his good hand over one ear but it didn't even come close to shutting out the sound.

thirteen

Benjy sat by himself in the living-room. Well, he wasn't quite by himself – Jonah was there, sleeping beside the sofa. Benjy kept thinking about the lost match. He looked at the ghost dog and said, "I'll be getting rid of you very soon."

Jonah stirred and opened one eye. He looked at Benjy as if to say, "Don't count on it. You didn't get rid of me last time, even though you made me jump off a cliff, remember?"

Benjy's dad came into the living-room. Mrs Harris and Kayla had gone to see an old friend of theirs, so it was just the two of them.

"Dad?" said Benjy.

"What is it?" he replied.

"How do you get rid of ghosts?"

His father laughed, as if it was a joke. When Benjy didn't laugh back, Andy sat beside him and said, "Are you getting bothered about Halloween or something? Are you scared? You don't need to be. There aren't really any ghosts. It's sort of like a game. People pretend. It's made up."

"Ghosts are real," said Benjy, looking at Jonah. Why couldn't his father see him? The mutt was wide awake now and scratching his left ear.

Andy came over and sat on the sofa beside him. "No one's ever caught a ghost or managed to take a picture of one, or at least, not a picture that proves anything. Some people say that ghosts are just in the minds of those that see them."

"It's not just in my mind."

"Is this about Jonah? Are you still thinking that he's in the house?"

"He *is* in the house. Why won't you believe me?"

"It's not that I don't believe you. I mean, I don't think you're just pretending—"

"Mrs Harris thinks I'm pretending." Benjy

was remembering all the times she'd been cross with him for even talking about Jonah. Only the other day, she'd said, "If you mention that dog one more time, I'll really lose my temper." Benjy watched as Jonah rubbed his back against the sofa. He was so close to his dad that Jonah's breath could have touched his bare foot. "Can't you feel anything?" asked Benjy.

"What should I be feeling?"

"Nothing," Benjy answered. What was the point? His dad would only think it was all in his head.

"Come and help me with the dinner, there's a good boy. Carol and Kayla will be home soon."

After they'd eaten, Benjy went back into the living-room. Maybe there was something about ghosts and how to get rid of them on the Internet. He switched on the computer. How do you spell ghost? he thought. Wasn't it one of those funny words that had an "h" in it that shouldn't be there? He remembered what Mrs Harris always said about words you couldn't spell: "Look it up in the dictionary." Benjy went to the bookshelf and found the one his father had given him ages ago. The catch was that, if you couldn't spell a word, it was hard to find it in a dictionary. Why hadn't Mrs Harris thought of that one? Benjy thought he was going to have to go through every g-word in the book, when he suddenly came across it – g-h-o-s-t. Why was spelling so stupid? There was no logic to it. He wrote "Ghost" very slowly on a piece of paper. His arm was out of the sling now but the weight of the plaster made his handwriting even worse than usual. Then he checked that he had each letter in exactly the right order.

There were thousands and thousands of Internet sites about ghosts but they didn't seem to have anything sensible to say about how you got rid of them. Benjy banged the desk with his fist, making the pencils rattle.

"Benjy! What are you doing?" Mrs Harris shouted from the kitchen.

"Nothing," Benjy shouted back crossly. She was always checking on him and interfering. It was like being at school twenty-four/seven, with no weekends or holidays.

Kayla came into the living-room. "What are you doing?" she said, echoing Mrs Harris.

"*Nothing,*" Benjy repeated.

"Why are you on the computer? Is this home-work? What's the site?"

"It's nothing."

Kayla picked up the piece of paper with "Ghost" written on it in Benjy's scrawly writing. "What's this?" she said.

"Nothing," said Benjy.

"Don't you get tired of saying the same word over and over?" asked Kayla.

"No. Nothing, nothing, nothing, nothing, nothing. See? I'm not at all tired yet."

"Don't get your knickers in a twist." Kayla walked over to the window and looked out. A firework went off, even though it was still only October. "Did you see that?" she said. "Does your dad do bonfires on Guy Fawkes? My dad used to."

Kayla's father, Mr Harris, had died when she was three. "Do you remember them?" asked Benjy.

"Of course I remember. 'Remember remember

the fifth of November,'" Kayla repeated quietly to herself.

"Do you miss your dad?"

Kayla shrugged again. "It was a long time ago," she said.

"I miss my mum," said Benjy. "She's gone to America. She doesn't phone me any more, and she doesn't send cards like she used to."

"I miss my dad," admitted Kayla.

They were silent for a moment, united by the things they shared. Then Benjy said, "I'm looking up 'Ghosts'."

Kayla squatted beside him. "Why?"

"You wouldn't believe me if I told you."

"I might. Is this still the Jonah thing?"

Benjy nodded.

"I haven't seen him, but I can feel him in the house," said Kayla. "He's sort of still here. I don't mind it though."

"He's angry with me," Benjy said.

"How do you know?"

"Wouldn't you be angry if I'd killed you? Anyway, he keeps doing things to get even. Bad things. I get the blame."

"What kind of things?"

"I keep telling people. That time the bathroom got all wet, that was Jonah. And he really did eat my homework. And when I fell off the chair, Jonah did that. He made City lose that match—"

"OK, OK. So all that was Jonah? You were telling the truth?"

Benjy nodded. "He wants to pay me back for that cliff. I have to get rid of him once and for all."

"Is he here now?"

Benjy looked around. He didn't appear to be. "I have to get rid of him once and for all though," Benjy repeated.

Kayla thought about this for a moment. "It can't be that nice for Jonah to have to stick around here. He probably doesn't want to be haunting you all the time. He'd probably rather be having a good long rest."

"He rests here. He goes to sleep by my bed at night. And he sleeps in front of the television."

"Dogs do sleep a lot," said Kayla. But he probably doesn't want to have to sleep here on earth."

"Where then?"

Kayla shrugged again. "I don't know. Wherever dogs go when their time comes. Just not here. There aren't supposed to be ghost dogs, are there? So it can't feel right for him either. We'll have to try to get him back to wherever he should be."

"How?"

"I don't know. We could ask Mum."

"She won't believe me. I asked Dad and he just thought I was nervous about Halloween. He gave me this talk about how there aren't any ghosts, no one's even managed to take a photo of one, but there are – Jonah proves it."

"That's it, Benjy! You have to take a photograph of Jonah. Then Mum and your dad will believe you and they'll help you get rid of him."

"I haven't got a camera."

"I have. I'll give you a lend of it if you like."

"Would you?"

"Sure. I'll go and get it now," said Kayla.

As she left, Benjy felt hopeful for the first time in ages. Kayla believed him and they were going to take a picture which would prove once and for all that Jonah really did exist.

fourteen

Benjy took loads of pictures of Jonah with Kayla's camera. He was sleeping in some of them, and running round the kitchen in others. Then Mrs Harris said that it was such a lovely afternoon that they should go to the park. Of course, Jonah went too, so Benjy photographed him there as well, using the flash as it began to get dark.

As they walked home, Benjy sniffed the air, just as Jonah was doing. It smelled sharp and fresh. Jonah began to run on ahead. He kept charging into the fallen leaves and whipping them up with his feet. They billowed up everywhere.

"It's windy this afternoon," said Mrs Harris.

"It's not the wind," said Benjy.

"What is it then?"

Benjy didn't answer. Instead, he ran with Jonah, kicking the leaves as he went and shouting at the top of his voice. Jonah barked excitedly as if to say, "Play with me, Benjy. Let's have some fun."

Benjy started to laugh. It was good having a dog, even if he was a ghost. He stood still again. He had just realized something. If the photos came out and he did manage to get rid of Jonah, life would be very dull indeed.

"Good dog, Jonah," shouted Benjy, knowing that his voice would be drowned by the sound of the wind. He ran with Jonah again, chasing him wildly through the trees.

When they got home, they found a note from Benjy's dad on the kitchen table. "He's had to go into work," said Mrs Harris as she read it.

"It's not fair!" said Benjy crossly. "Dad promised he'd help me write a letter to Mum tonight."

Benjy looked so sad that Mrs Harris said, "I'll help you do it, Benjy. We could have a go now, if you like."

Benjy almost said that he didn't want any help

from her, he wanted his dad, but he saw that Mrs Harris was only being kind so he nodded instead and went to get some paper and a pen.

It took ages to write the letter because the plaster weighed so much and the handwriting was terrible, but Mrs Harris didn't tell him off once.

"Why don't you tell your mum all about the photos you were taking earlier?" said Mrs Harris.

Benjy started to write again. "How do you spell 'photograph'?" he said.

On the morning that the photographs were ready for collection, Benjy lay in bed staring at the ceiling. It was almost six o'clock and no one else was up. He tiptoed to Kayla's room and knocked on the door, but there was no answer. She was probably still asleep. He went in and sat at the foot of her bed. She was obviously dreaming of something nice. She was smiling. Every now and then, she made a little chuckling sound. Still, he had to wake her up. Now that it was nearly Halloween, he really needed her help or they could be in a load of trouble.

As if he knew that Benjy was thinking about him, Jonah appeared. He jumped on to the seat in the corner of Kayla's room and settled down on it. He soon fell asleep and started to snore. Benjy was amazed that Kayla didn't wake up, and then he realized he was being silly. Kayla still couldn't see or hear Jonah. He was always the only one who knew the dog was there. Benjy got up and stood by Kayla's pillow. "Wake up," he said, shaking her shoulder.

Kayla opened one eye and looked at him. "What do you want? What time is it?"

"It's still early."

"Why did you wake me? I was having such a good dream. I'd just won a drawing competition and the prize was the biggest ice-cream sundae you've ever seen and a trip to Disney World…"

"It was just a dream. I want to talk to you about something real. It's photograph day."

Kayla sat up then. "Of course it is. But try to stay calm about it."

"What if the pictures don't come out?"

Kayla said what her mother always said in

such situations. "We'll cross that bridge when we come to it."

Jonah gave an extra loud snore, causing Benjy to jump so high that he almost fell off the bed.

"I told you to stay calm," said Kayla.

"Didn't you hear it?"

"Was it Jonah? Did he do something? You know I can't hear him. I wish I could."

"Do you really wish it?"

"More than anything. I'd love to see him again."

Benjy went over to the chair where Jonah was sleeping, causing him to wake up. He looked at Benjy as if he was pleased to see him. Benjy sat beside him on the chair and began to speak to him in a low voice. "Listen, mate, can't you let Kayla see you? I bet you could do it if you really tried. Come on, Jonah. She really, really wants to. It isn't fair that I'm the only one who ever gets to know you're here. Please let her see you, please, Jonah." But nothing happened except that Jonah closed his eyes again and went back to sleep.

Benjy stood up. "It isn't any good," he said.

"I don't think he's even listening."

Kayla looked so disappointed that Benjy started to think he'd got it all wrong. He'd thought Jonah was a kind of punishment, but maybe that wasn't true at all. Benjy had been so miserable when his dad and Mrs Harris had got married. And it had been even worse when Mrs Harris and Kayla had actually moved in. They all had each other and he'd been left with nobody. And then Jonah had started appearing and it had been as if he had a friend. And because Jonah was a ghost dog, he'd even been around at school, sitting under Benjy's desk and keeping him company, and entertaining him during the most boring lessons. Benjy had never really had any friends at school. His bad temper put most people off so they never bothered to get to know him. Jonah had taken the trouble to get to know him properly. And the funny thing was, now that they were used to each other, Jonah seemed to like what he saw. He stuck with Benjy even though he'd caused the accident on the cliff and, in a funny kind of way, he made him feel a whole lot better. It was a shame that Kayla couldn't see him too. She would have loved it.

"I'm sorry," Benjy said. "I thought he'd let you see him."

"Never mind," answered Kayla. "Thanks for trying."

"You still believe me though, don't you? You still believe he's here?"

"Yes, I still believe you. You haven't got enough imagination to be making all this up."

Benjy tried to think of a sarky reply but he couldn't so he gave up and smiled instead. Kayla was so good at insults that he couldn't keep up with her most of the time. But she was funny with it, and he couldn't help laughing even though he didn't want to.

"You look quite nice when you smile or laugh," said Kayla. "You should try to exercise your face a bit more."

Benjy pulled a face at her. "Is that enough exercise for you?" he said. This time, Kayla failed to think of a sarky reply and they smiled at one another. "Tell you what though," added Benjy. "I'll really be smiling if those photos come out right. I'll probably be famous and everything."

*   *   *

The photographs didn't come out right though. In each one, there was just an empty space where Jonah should have been. As Benjy and Kayla went through the batch that Mrs Harris brought home from Boots, they could have cried with disappointment.

"Never mind," said Mrs Harris. "They're just over-exposed or something. What were they meant to be pictures of?"

"Nothing," said Benjy.

"Come on, it's not the end of the world."

Benjy perked up a little. Maybe she was right. After all, only that morning he'd been thinking that he wouldn't mind if Jonah stayed. It was fun to have a dog, even if he was a ghost. Benjy stroked Jonah gently as Mrs Harris went outside to do a bit of gardening.

fifteen

Benjy was sitting in Kayla's room. For once, he was already dressed and ready for school. They were doing a jigsaw puzzle together while they waited for Mrs Harris. Benjy had thought it would be boring, but he was discovering that he was good at puzzles. He had an eye for shape and colour, and he was quicker than Kayla at working out which piece should go where. This pleased him. He hadn't been able to beat Kayla at anything much until now.

Benjy looked up and caught sight of Jonah. He was slumped in a chair. His coat looked dull and he was breathing too quickly. Benjy hurried over to him again. "I think there's something wrong with Jonah," he said.

"Of course there's something wrong with him. He's dead," said Kayla.

"No, I mean he's changed, he's not the same as usual. He's all mopey, he's just lying there. And his tail isn't wagging. It used to wag all the time. What do you think's wrong?"

Kayla thought about it. Then she said, "He shouldn't be here, haunting you, should he? I mean, other dogs, when they die, they don't come back to earth, do they? They don't appear to people. I think it's some kind of a mistake, and it's starting to make him miserable."

This made sense to Benjy. "What can we do about it?" he asked.

"I don't know, but let me have a think. I'll let you know once I have a plan."

Kayla was so bossy. It wasn't up to her to have a plan, it was up to him, decided Benjy. "I'm going to think of a plan. He's sort of my dog now."

"He isn't your dog."

"He is. You can't see him, only I can see him. It's me he's haunting, not you." Benjy looked at Jonah once more. He seemed really ill. He was hunched up and his eyes were watering. "There's something very wrong with him," Benjy said.

"We have to make him better," answered Kayla.

Benjy nodded. There was no point in squabbling about who should figure out a plan. All that mattered was making sure Jonah was OK, and getting him back to where he ought to be. So Benjy said, "We'll think of a plan together. You know what your mum would say – two heads are better than one."

"Benjy! Kayla! Time to go to school," Mrs Harris shouted from downstairs.

"OK!" they called together.

"Look, let's meet at break near the football pitch," said Benjy.

"All right," replied Kayla.

"And don't stop thinking. We're going to need every thought we've got if we're going to put things right for Jonah."

Benjy yawned. Mrs Harris was going on and on about how the class should learn to think about other people and not just about themselves. Benjy peered under the desk and saw that Jonah was yawning too. That made him smile.

"Why are you looking so pleased with yourself, Benjy?" asked Mrs Harris, though she said it quite kindly.

It was then that Benjy had a really brilliant idea. He decided to tell everyone about it. "It's Halloween next week. On Halloween, everyone goes round to people's houses trick or treating, don't they?" he said. "Only, what if this Halloween, we all went round in our costumes and collected money to give to a charity?"

Mrs Harris smiled. "That is a good idea, Benjy," she said. "Which charity were you thinking of?"

"A dog charity."

"Like the dogs' home?"

"Yes, the dogs' home would be brilliant." Benjy felt sure that Jonah would approve. It might even make him get better.

At break, Benjy met Kayla, as planned, by the football pitch. She was sitting on the bench looking miserable.

"What's up?" asked Benjy.

"I haven't been able to think of a plan," she

said, so Benjy told her about the collection he was going to make. "And you'll come too, won't you?"

"Isn't it just your class?"

"Yes, but you can bring family."

Kayla was pleased Benjy thought of her as family, but then she said, "I'm not being mean or anything, but I don't know if the collection will be enough. I think Jonah needs something else as well, but I'm not sure what. Why don't we go and talk to Mum? She might have some ideas."

"She doesn't believe in Jonah."

"She'd still try to help, honest."

"No, she'll just tell me to stop being silly."

"She won't now. She knows you better. And she knows you're not pretending. Come on, she'll be in your classroom."

Kayla tried to take Benjy's hand, but he wouldn't let her – the other boys might have seen. But he ran with her across the playground and biffed her every now and then – not hard at all, it was just a game – and she biffed him back. They reached the classroom laughing and shouting. Jonah trailed behind.

Mrs Harris looked up with an irritated expression. She was hoping to eat her dinner in peace. But then she noticed that Kayla and Benjy were looking serious about something so she put down her cheese and Marmite sandwiches with a little sigh and said, "What's up, you two?"

Benjy picked up one of the sandwiches and sniffed it. "How can you eat cheese and Marmite together? It smells disgusting."

"It's a delicacy," she said. "An acquired taste for sophisticated people."

Benjy didn't know what she was talking about. He perched on one of the tables, pulling Kayla up beside him.

"Mum," said Kayla, "you know that Benjy sees Jonah, and you know that he's really serious and he isn't pretending?"

Mrs Harris nodded. "I'm not saying I believe that Jonah's here, but I can see now that you do, Benjy, and I'm sorry I got cross about it. At first, I thought you were making it up just to be annoying."

"I wasn't!" Benjy protested hotly.

"I know you weren't. That's what I'm saying."

"Benjy says that Jonah's not right. I think he's gone funny because he needs to go to wherever dogs end up when they die. How would we get him there?"

"Now you're asking," Mrs Harris answered.

"It's really important, Mum."

"I know. I just need to think about it. I'm not very well informed about ghosts."

This surprised Benjy. He'd thought that Mrs Harris knew everything.

"Leave it with me and we'll talk some more on the way home this evening."

Benjy nodded. "OK. Thanks."

"Thanks, Mum," said Kayla.

As they were going through the door, Mrs Harris said, "Benjy? Your idea about collecting for the dog's home on Halloween was a very good and thoughtful one."

Benjy felt himself blush. Usually, no one praised him for anything, and he was very pleased. So was Jonah. He gave his tail a feeble wag and followed Benjy slowly out of the room.

* * *

That evening, in the car, Mrs Harris said to Benjy, "I've given some thought to the problem with Jonah. Do you think that if we gave him a proper send-off it would help?"

"What do you mean, a proper send-off?" asked Benjy.

"She means bury him," said Kayla.

"Not quite, because to have a burial you need a body and we don't have one. But we could go into the garden and put a few flowers by Jonah's favourite tree and say some nice things about him. It could be a memorial ceremony, which just means remembering someone and saying goodbye to them. If we said goodbye to Jonah properly, he might know that it was time to leave you, Benjy. What do you think?"

"It might work," said Benjy. "And I think we should do it on Halloween, after the collection for the dogs' home. I'm sure Halloween would be the right day."

"Halloween it is then," said Mrs Harris with a smile.

sixteen

After school on the evening of Halloween, Benjy rushed into the house, calling for his dad. There was no answer. Benjy turned to Mrs Harris and Kayla and said, "He promised he'd get home early to take us out. He promised."

Mrs Harris said, "There's still plenty of time, Benjy. You're not going out for at least another hour. I'm sure Andy will be back by then."

"He'd better be."

"Benjy, your dad's work is important to him and it's not something he can just drop. If somebody needs him, he has to be there."

"I need him."

"I know you do, Benjy, and he really loves you and needs you too."

"Then why isn't he here?"

"He will be. Listen, I've finished your Halloween costumes. Don't say I never do anything for you, OK? I was sewing until after two o'clock this morning."

"Where are they?" asked Kayla, jumping up and down.

"In your bedrooms."

Benjy and Kayla ran upstairs. There, on Benjy's bed, was a red demon costume in soft velvet, complete with pointy ears and a pitchfork made from papier-mâché.

"*Cool,*" said Benjy. He'd been worried that he'd have to wear something cute rather than scary, like a pumpkin outfit. "What have you got, Kayla?" he called.

"I'm a bat!" said Kayla, bursting into Benjy's room in a black costume with little wings and a tail.

Benjy put his outfit on and they stood side by side, admiring themselves in the mirror.

"What does Jonah think?" asked Kayla.

"He thinks we look magnificent," Benjy replied, though Jonah was actually fast asleep on Benjy's bed. "Do you think the memorial thing will work?"

Kayla nodded. "If Mum thinks it will, it will," she said.

"Mrs Harris is OK," said Benjy. "Or at least, she's OK when she isn't being a teacher."

"Benjy," said Kayla, "do you think you could try calling her Carol? It's really odd hearing you call her Mrs Harris all the time."

Benjy nodded, though he couldn't imagine using her first name. He decided he'd try to avoid calling her anything in future. "Dad still isn't here," he said. "He's never here. It isn't fair. What if he doesn't get home in time to go out with us? Your mum can't do it, she's visiting that friend of hers in hospital."

"He'll come home soon, I bet you. Like Mum said, he's very busy."

Benjy nodded. "Tell me about it," he replied.

It was fish fingers and spaghetti hoops for tea – one of Benjy's favourites – but he didn't enjoy it because he was listening out for his dad. There was only a quarter of an hour left before they had to meet the other children from Benjy's class. Mrs Harris had her coat on, ready to see her friend.

"He still isn't here," said Benjy. At that moment, the phone rang. Benjy ran and picked it up. "It's Dad," he said. "Where are you?" he asked his father. "You're not still at work, are you?" Benjy turned to Mrs Harris. "He wants to talk to you," he said.

Mrs Harris took the phone. "I've got to go in a minute, I can't let Tracy down, she's just had her operation and I promised I'd go tonight. There isn't anyone else, she'll be on her own... No, I can't, Andy. You said you'd be here. It's not fair on me, and it's not fair on the kids. They're in their costumes and everything."

"He isn't coming home, is he?" said Benjy, tugging on Mrs Harris's sleeve.

"Just a minute, Benjy, I'm trying to talk... Andy, I know you can't leave this kid, but what about your own son? You've got to be more assertive, tell that boss of yours to sort the problem out himself... I know... Yes, I do know, Andy... OK, I'll see you later then." Mrs

Harris put down the phone.

"He isn't coming, is he?" said Benjy once more.

"He's been delayed. A boy ran away this afternoon and your dad had to go and fetch him — there wasn't anybody else. Now he's stuck on the other side of Manchester."

"Great," said Benjy. "He's going to spoil this. I made collection tins for the dogs' home and everything. I was really looking forward to it."

"I'm sure you can still go. I'll nip next door and ask Mrs Jenkins to take you with Steven. I'm sure it won't be a problem."

"Can't me and Kayla go by ourselves?"

"No, you can't, you're too young and it isn't safe. I'll be back in a minute."

When Mrs Harris returned, she said, "You're in luck. Pam Jenkins is happy to have you tag along with them. After that, we'll do the memorial ceremony for Jonah."

"You will come back in time for it, won't you? Even if your friend's really ill? It's important for Jonah. We've got to do it on Halloween. That's what he wants, I'm sure it is."

"I'll be back in plenty of time. Your dad will be home too, I'm sure."

"You're not sure or you wouldn't be saying 'I'm sure'. People always say 'I'm sure' when they're not sure about something."

"Sharp as tack," said Mrs Harris. "I'm *nearly* sure, all right? Come on, let's go next door. Pam and Steven are waiting for you."

"Did you make those costumes for the children, Carol?" Pam Jenkins said as they all arrived on her doorstep. "They're fantastic, you're so clever. I'm useless. Poor Steven never looks right for these things."

Steven's costume was just a sheet with a face painted on it and a couple of holes for eyes so that he could see. It was meant to be a ghost. "It's fine, Pam," said Mrs Harris. "Steven looks very nice."

He doesn't, he looks hopeless, thought Benjy but, for once, he kept his thoughts to himself.

"Are we all set, then?" asked Pam. "Lead the way, Benjy. I like your collection tin. You should get lots of money for the dogs' home."

Benjy smiled. Jonah, who was beside him as usual, wagged his tail in approval. It was the first sign of a wag that Benjy had seen all day. They really had to give Jonah his send-off very soon. He was getting so slow and miserable that he was becoming a different dog.

"Can I carry the tin?" asked Kayla.

Benjy was about to say no and then he remembered how helpful Kayla had been lately, and that she'd believed him about Jonah when no one else had done. So he handed her the tin with barely a word of protest.

"I feel stupid," said Steven. "Everyone's going to laugh at me."

"No they won't," said Benjy, though he secretly thought that they probably would. "Look, the others are over there!" he shouted as they reached the corner of the street. "Charlotte's got a witch's outfit. And Connor's an owl, like in *Harry Potter*."

The children were split into several small groups, each led by one of the parents. The collecting went very well. Most of the neighbours gave money and said it was a really good idea. Benjy started to glow with pride and happiness, and Jonah perked up a little.

After an hour or two, they'd knocked at

almost every house in the neighbourhood. Mrs Jenkins stayed on the step of number 49, talking to her friend Mrs Anfield. "We're just going up there," Steven called to her, pointing up the street. He was getting cold just standing around. "Let's knock at that red house. We haven't done that one yet," he said.

"We should wait for your mum," said Kayla.

"You don't know what she's like when her and Mrs Anfield get together. They'll be there all night," said Steven.

"Come on," said Benjy. "Steven's mum can still see us. What could happen? We'll be fine."

There was a light on at the red house but no one answered the knock at the door.

"They're out," said Kayla. "They probably left the light on to stop burglars."

"How much money have we got altogether?" asked Steven.

"I don't know," answered Benjy.

"Count it," said Kayla.

Benjy sat on the step and began to sort through the coins. They were all so occupied with figuring out how much they'd collected that they didn't notice Paul Fish coming towards them until it was too late.

Paul stood over Benjy and said, "You've come into a lot of money all of a sudden."

"It's a collection. It's for charity," said Kayla. "It's for the dogs' home, if you must know. Why don't you put some money in?"

"Mouthy, isn't she?" Paul said to no one in particular. "And look at him," he added, pointing to Steven. "Your costume's rubbish. You look a complete banana."

Steven wriggled uncomfortably under his sheet. He was glad that no one could actually see him blushing.

"And what are you supposed to be?" Paul asked Benjy.

"Can't you tell?"

"Well, you're red and round. You must be a tomato!"

"Don't be stupid!" said Benjy, forgetting for a moment that Paul was a lot bigger than he was.

"Don't call me stupid," said Paul. "For that, you can give me that money. You have to pay people compensation when you say something bad about them that isn't true. My dad told me. So pay up."

"You *are* stupid," said Benjy.

Paul scooped up some of the coins and dropped them in his pocket.

"That's stealing!" Kayla said.

"Shut up, Mouth," said Paul. "It isn't stealing, it's compensation, like I told you. For that, I'll have the rest as well." He gathered up the remaining money and started running towards the end of the road.

"Give it back, it isn't yours!" yelled Benjy. He ran after Paul.

"Don't, Benjy. Just tell Mrs Jenkins," shouted Kayla.

But Mrs Jenkins was barely in sight, and she was still deep in conversation with her friend, so Benjy continued to chase the bigger boy. He had shorter legs but he could run like a whippet when he felt like it, even with a broken arm, and he really felt like it now. He was angry. He kept thinking about all the homeless dogs and how their food money was being nicked. And he also thought about Jonah, who was following close behind, but much more slowly than usual. Kayla and Steven were following too.

Benjy caught the tail of Paul's jacket and held on tight. Paul tried to shake him off, but Benjy was determined. When Paul saw that he couldn't get rid of Benjy so easily, he slapped him hard on the nose. Benjy let go of the jacket for a moment and rubbed his nose, wondering if it would start to bleed, but then he grabbed hold of the jacket again, even more tightly than before. His bad arm began to ache with the effort. "Give us back our money!" he shouted.

"Make me!" said Paul, hitting out once more. Benjy ducked so Paul missed this time.

"Pick on someone your own size!" said Steven, looking round for his mother. But, in chasing Paul, they'd all gone further than he'd thought, and now Mrs Jenkins was nowhere to be seen.

Paul hit out again and caught Benjy in the chest. He started to wheeze. This time he had no choice but to let go of the jacket for good, but Paul was still raging. He lashed out again, wanting to teach Benjy a lesson but, before he could connect with Benjy's stomach, Steven deliberately stepped forward and caught the blow instead. It knocked him to his knees. Kayla tried to grab Paul's arm but he shook her off easily.

It was then that Benjy saw Jonah gather all the strength he had. He hurled himself at Paul, making him fall to the ground. Benjy, breathless and aching, took the opportunity to gather up the money and shove it back in the collection tin.

"What are you doing?" shouted Mrs Jenkins. She had just realized what was going on. "Clear off at once! How dare you hit younger children! I'll be reporting you to your head teacher tomorrow." She turned to Benjy. "I saw you trip up that big lad after he'd hit you. That was brave. Are you OK?"

Benjy almost said that it wasn't him who'd tripped Paul, it was Jonah, but then he remembered that there was no point – no one would believe him. "Kayla and Steven helped," said Benjy. "They were brave too." He looked at Steven respectfully, and Steven glowed.

Benjy and Steven linked arms, pleased with themselves and with each other. Then Benjy looked down, expecting to see Jonah wagging his tail, but the ghost dog was lying on the ground, panting heavily. He looked worse than ever.

"We have to get home," whispered Benjy to Kayla. "Jonah was the one who tackled Paul and it's worn him out. We've got to get him back where he belongs."

"All right," said Kayla. "Mum should be back by now, and your dad. Let's go and get the memorial thing over with and then, hopefully, Jonah will end up where he really belongs."

seventeen

By the time Kayla and Benjy got home it was almost half past eight. Mrs Harris had just got in too and she was taking off her coat in the hall. Andy's jacket wasn't on its peg, so Benjy knew that he was still out. "It's not fair," he muttered crossly to himself.

Kayla tweaked his sleeve. "He can't help it, Ben. He just isn't an on-time sort of person."

"Tell me about it," Benjy replied.

Mrs Harris said, "I think we'd better put Jonah's send-off on hold. It can wait a day or two. It's quite late now and you're both very tired. And your dad isn't home yet either, Benjy."

"I know he isn't. And it isn't—"

"*Fair*," chorused Kayla and her mother.

"Shut up!" said Benjy. He didn't want to join in with their laughter but he couldn't help himself and suddenly they were all laughing until they felt weak. "It wasn't even all that funny," said Benjy, breathlessly. "And our money for the dogs' home nearly got pinched and Paul Fish tried to bash us up and now you're telling me we can't even say goodbye to Jonah tonight."

Benjy stopped laughing as he realized what this could mean. "It's Halloween. It has to be tonight. It won't work tomorrow. Things like this definitely have to happen on Halloween. Please, you promised. I know Dad isn't here but we could do it without him. We have to do it now, we really have to."

Mrs Harris could see that Benjy really meant it so she sighed and said, "OK then. Put your outdoor things back on. We'll need to go into the garden." She began to put on her coat again. "There are some candles in the living-room and some flowers too. I bought them this dinner time. And I thought we could sing something.

What do you think would be good, Benjy?"

Benjy remembered an old song that his mother used to sing to him. "'How Much is that Doggy in the Window?' That's a good song and Jonah would like it."

"I was thinking of something a bit more … *special* than that," said Mrs Harris.

"We could do 'Who Let the Dogs Out?'," said Kayla. "Or there's that song that goes 'give a dog a bone' in the chorus."

Mrs Harris gave up. "OK, we'll start with 'How Much is that Doggy?' and then go on to 'Who Let the Dogs Out?'"

Benjy looked down at Jonah, who had staggered along behind him all the way home. "He seems pleased with that," he said.

"Put your wellies on as well. And take your gloves. I don't want anyone off school next week with a cold."

Benjy put on his trainers and left his gloves on the chair in the hall. Being off school sounded pretty good to him. "Come on then, Jonah," he said as he opened the back door and ran into the garden. Jonah followed at his slowest pace.

Kayla was carrying the flowers and Mrs Harris had the candles. She gave one to each of the children and lit them with a taper. She lit one for herself as well. The dim light flickered across the garden, casting strange shadows. They could see a pile of stones by the cherry tree.

"I thought we'd make that Jonah's tree," said Mrs Harris. "And those are his memorial stones. It's like a little rockery."

"Whenever we trip over them, we can think of Jonah," said Benjy. They all laughed again, even though it was a solemn moment.

Mrs Harris began to sing "How Much is that Doggy in the Window?" Kayla and Benjy joined in. And then there was another voice, a loud man's voice, singing the chorus, and Benjy turned and saw that his dad was home. They smiled at one another. Benjy gave Andy his candle and picked up the flowers. He held them tight.

"I thought we could bury Jonah's lead," said Mrs Harris. "It would be a nice gesture to bury something as we had to leave Jonah at the bottom of the cliff."

Benjy nodded. "I'll do it," he said. As he dug the little hole with the garden trowel, Benjy thought of Jonah running along that cliff. He thought how excited the dog had been that day, and how happy. And somehow, the excited, happy spirit of Jonah had stayed with Benjy, cheering him up and helping him to get on with Carol and Kayla. And Benjy knew that it hadn't been sad or frightening or terrible to be haunted by a dog, it had been funny and friendly and it had made him feel warm inside.

"Time to say goodbye now," said Benjy to the small figure of a dog who was lying beside him. And even as Benjy said it, Jonah started to fade very slowly, like the Cheshire Cat. And then he was gone.

Kayla reached out and held Benjy's hand. He dropped the collar into the hole he'd made and covered it with earth. Then he turned and hurried into the house.

That night, as he lay in bed, Benjy was surrounded by howling dogs. The sound was unearthly. They closed in on him, with their fur standing on end. Benjy began to tremble and then he started to cry, but Jonah ran into the midst of the scary dogs and drove them all away.

"Wake up, Benjy, it's only a dream!" Benjy awoke to find Carol standing over him. "It's all right, it isn't real," she said.

"Jonah was chasing away the horrible dogs," said Benjy. "It's because it's Halloween. They've come to scare me."

"It was just a dream," repeated Carol. "You don't need to be scared."

"It seemed really real, but Jonah saved me. Do you think he's happy now, Carol?"

"I'm sure he is," she said.

Benjy felt under his pillow for the letter he'd written to his mother with Carol's help. He hadn't posted it yet.

"I'm not going to see my mum again, am I?" he said.

"Of course you are, Benjy."

"Mum can't afford to come here and Dad is always so busy, he won't be able to take me to America."

"Your dad *will* take you. You'll go with him

next summer, I promise. I'll make sure of it."

Benjy looked at her to check that she really meant it and saw that she did. It felt nice to have her sitting on his bed, holding his hand when he'd had a bad dream. It was like having a mother again. Benjy stopped the thought as soon as it was in his head. No one could replace his real mother. No one, not ever. But his real mum was far away in America and he hardly saw her any more, and Carol was around instead. It was like when City lost a player to injury. They got a substitute. And maybe it wasn't the best footballer or the one you really wanted to see play in the match, but you had to make the best of things. That was just how it was.

"Go back to sleep again, Benjy. Everything will seem a lot better in the morning," Carol said.

Benjy's eyes closed and he began to drift off to sleep again. In his dreams, he and Jonah played until they couldn't play any more, and the dog got the biggest pile of bones in the whole universe and he chased a huge red ball that he always managed to catch before it went over any cliffs.

*   *   *